# CONSIDER
# PEGASUS

## A SPACE TALE ABOUT UNICORN RIGHTS

## PRAISE FOR THE LEFT HAND OF DOG

A deeply heartfelt story ... Clarke understands the peculiar magic that is addressing a serious topic without taking oneself seriously in the process, and wields wit and wordplay with enviable skill. Pratchett and Adams fans, take note.

Wonderfully charming and beautifully weird... I can't stop thinking about how delightful this book is. It is exactly what I needed!

It didn't take me long to realise I would absolutely love this novel.

If you like alien first contact, nerdy references, and talking dogs – you wanna read this book!

Farcical theatre at its best ... full of wit and charm.

A wonderfully accessible yarn.

What a fun book!

A perfect way to spend a stormy evening.

# CONSIDER PEGASUS

## A SPACE TALE ABOUT UNICORN RIGHTS

### STARSHIP TEAPOT #3

### SI CLARKE

Print edition ISBN 978-1-7397681-2-6

ebook edition ISBN 978-1-7397681-1-9

Consider Pegasus

www.whitehartfiction.co.uk

Most recent update: 15 November 2022

Editing by:

- Charlie Knight of Charlie Knight Writes

- Nicholas Taylor of Just Write Right

- Hannah McCall of Black Cat Editorial Services

Cover art by: Rebeca Covers

Teapot illustration by: Yuliya Zabelina

Unicorn horn illustration by: Ryan Prakoso

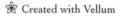 Created with Vellum

## AUTHOR'S NOTE

This book is written in British English. If you're used to reading American English, some of the spelling and punctuation may seem unusual. I promise, it's totally safe.

This story also features a number of Canadianisms. Sadly, I cannot promise these are safe. You may find yourself involuntarily wearing a touque and craving Timbits and a double-double. It can't be helped. Seek treatment immediately.

Lastly, this book contains an inordinate number of geek culture references. This as an homage to all things science fiction. There are countless references to all my favourites – *Star Trek*, *Red Dwarf*, *Firefly*, *The X-Files*, *Doctor Who*, *Battlestar Galactica*, *Hitchhiker's Guide to the Galaxy*, *Babylon 5*, *The Expanse*, etc. None of it should be read as derogatory or dismissive, nor would I ever suggest my work can take the place of anyone else's. Please support artists and authors. This is my love song to the entire genre.

## CONTENT WARNINGS

- Strong themes of ableism and transphobia throughout
- Pregnancy and brief mentions of miscarriage and baby loss

Also, please note that trans women are women. Trans men are men. Non-binary people are who they tell you they are. This book is not for TERFs.

*PREVIOUSLY ON STARSHIP
TEAPOT...*

Okay, you know how in TV shows you get that little one-minute segment at the start of each episode to catch you up? Books should do that too, I think. Just a handy little reminder since it may have been a while since you read the previous books. Or maybe you're like me and you've jumped right in at book three. No judgement.

––––––

Previously on *Starship Teapot*... [You may want to imagine Anthony Stewart Head's voice reading this to you.]

Lem, a perfectly ordinary aro-ace agender IT project manager, is kidnapped by aliens while camping with her German shepherd, Spock. While trying to figure out how to get home, they make some new friends: a talking horse-person, an unswearing robot, an overly anxious parrot, and a cloud of sentient glitter gas. Along the way, Lem discovers that the universe is far stranger than she'd ever imagined.

One of the things Lem learns is that Darmok and Jalad were right: communication requires a shared frame of reference. So, Holly, Lem's universal translator and personal AI, suggests using figurative mode to facilitate easier discourse.

*'This will include facts you already know but may have forgotten,' it explained. 'I will also incorporate extrapolative and fictional sources. Your extensive knowledge of science fiction will provide a useful base for figurative mode.'*

Early on in her new life in space, Lem encounters an alien.

*She raised her arms.* Wait, his arms? Their arms? *I shook my head. Not the time to wonder about alien pronouns. I decided to stick with* she *until someone told me otherwise.*

Much later, Lem learns that alien sex and gender are … complicated. The binary most people are used to on Earth doesn't apply.

*'Hang on,' I said. 'If pronouns don't align to sex or gender because most species don't think that way … does that mean BB, Aurora, and Henry aren't women?'*

So there are two pronouns: *she* for all sentient beings and *it* for all non-sentient/inanimate objects. And as for names…

*'Back in the early days of translators, programmers tried to transliterate names of people and places,' said Bexley. 'But it was all "unintelligible noise this" and "awkward silence that". No, in the end, they decided the best thing for it was for people to make their own names for everyone they encounter. Once you assign a name to some- one, your AI will remember it.'*

That's right: it's literally impossible to misgender or dead-name someone. Whatever you may call a person, the trans-lator will convert it to their preferred name or pronoun.

After two kidnappings and three escapes, Lem and the gang meet up in the pub. And when it's finally time to go home, Lem and Spock decide that, actually, they're more at home in this weird and wonderful universe than they ever were on Earth.

Lem and her new friends buy the *Teapot* and form a transport company. One of their first jobs is working for the Galactic Union (basically the space version of the EU). They're hired to help rescue people called the plenties before their planet is destroyed by an asteroid. Along the way, they meet the kobolds, a second species on the planet, who are oppressed by the plenties.

*Bexley emphasised each word with gestures. 'Okay, I have to preface this by saying I'm not a lawyer or anything. I know a little bit – and one thing I know for certain is that protecting people from slavery and oppression is a core tenet of the GU.'*

The Teapotters work alongside the kobolds, getting them off the planet before disaster strikes.

———

And now … the next episode.

# 1 / A SALAD PLATE?

'I still can't believe you two walked all that way in the dark.' Bexley heaved another crate into the getoff, the big ground-to-orbit vehicle we were loading. She had swiftly become my best friend in my new life in the Galactic Union. She looked a bit like a small chestnut-coloured horse on two legs with orange eyes and a long, blond mane.

I shrugged. 'It wasn't a big deal. Spock looked after me. She could see where we were going somehow.' I smiled at my German shepherd as the clouds above obscured the planet's distant sun. It wasn't exactly bright out – but this was as good as it got around here. I shuddered – I couldn't wait to see the back of this place. 'Well, no. She couldn't *see*. I've no idea how she could tell where we were. But she could. She kept me on the road.'

Spock raised her head. 'Spock good girl?' She couldn't help carry crates but she accompanied us everywhere as we loaded up. She and I had been kidnapped from Earth more than six months earlier in a case of mistaken identity.

Smiling, I buried my hand in her thick fur. 'The bestest, mate.'

Before heading back to grab the next crate, Bexley stopped to stroke Spock's nose. 'We couldn't ask for a better physical protection officer.'

Spock lay down on her back, one leg kicking in the air. 'Rub belly?'

Of course, both Bexley and I obliged.

With one hoof still on Spock, Bexley looked up at me. 'What about you, Lem? Are you feeling more settled now that you have specific responsibilities on the *Teapot*?'

For the first few months of our new life in space, I was uneasy. I knew I belonged and I felt welcomed and accepted – yet I didn't feel like I had a purpose of my own. But during our work evacuating the residents of planet Dave last month, it became apparent that my experience as a project manager on Earth could actually be useful in my new life. I breathed in the planet's stale, dusty air. After coughing most of it back up again, I replied. 'Yeah. I am. It feels good to add value. I like being productive. It's got me feeling more settled now.'

Bexley stood back up. 'Good. I'm glad. I mean, obviously, I'm not glad that you think you weren't being productive before. Because you totally were. And even if you weren't … we value you for who you *are*, not for what you can do for us.'

I pursed my lips. 'I know. But I suppose I've always been a bit … I don't know. The odd one out, I guess. No matter where I went or who I was with, part of me always felt like I didn't really fit in, you know?' It was tough to articulate what it was like to be just a little bit out of place all the time. Or a lot out of place. Depending.

Bexley chewed the air for a moment. 'I know. Believe me, I get that. I —'

Whatever Bexley was going to say next died away as

Henry rolled up to us pushing a trolley full of crates. 'Hey, meat-based people.'

Henry was a smooth blue cylinder who looked a bit like a vacuum. Or a rubbish bin. Her incredibly refined and cultured voice always seemed at odds with her insults and sarcasm.

'Hi, Henry,' said Bexley. 'We're going to make it on time, right?'

Henry extruded a pair of pointy implements and jabbed them at the crates. 'If you muffler parkas could stop taking breaks and hurry up with the loading, we will. The client said the frolicking job was ours so long as we got there by the end of the day. At warp five, we'll be there with a few corking hours to spare.'

Henry was unable to overwrite the programming that prevented her from swearing. But she always found ways to make her meaning clear.

'Sweet.' Bexley hoisted up one of Henry's crates and hauled it into the getoff. 'We'll get to Hard Rock station and collect the merchandise and... Oh my gosh! I've just remembered all over again what this job is. Have you ever even seen Galactovision? We're going to be carrying gear for Megaboulder! Like, we actually get to meet Megaboulder. And she's trusted us to transport her equipment to her next gig. Do you know how cool that is? I mean, seriously?'

Bexley and Aurora had both been gushing about this for days. From what I could gather, Galactovision was essentially Space Eurovision. The horta won last year with their entry, Megaboulder and the Accountants of Doom. Megaboulder and her band were capitalising on their fame with a galaxy-spanning tour. I was cautiously excited to see what Galactovision was all about – but so far it was a complete mystery.

We were loading the last of Henry's crates into the getoff

when BB and Aurora approached, steering another trolley with two crates.

I smiled at both of them. 'Hey, you two.'

BB lifted her golden yellow wings in greeting.

'Hello, everyone,' said Aurora.

Spock ran to meet them – well, Aurora mainly. 'Food friend! Bring Spock treats?'

BB reached out with her lower set of hands and ran her talons through Spock's fur. 'I'm pretty sure you've eaten recently.'

Spock's face fell. 'Spock not eat today. Starving.'

Aurora glowed royal blue and her nebulous form sort of quivered. 'That's simply not true.' She extended a gassy nub of herself and tickled Spock's chin.

Spock wagged her tail hopefully. 'Feed Spock?'

I hustled over to where they stood to break the cycle. Spock could play this game all day. 'Come here, sweetie.' I put my hand on her back and steered her back towards the getoff.

Bexley sort of ran-skipped over to BB and Aurora and waved a hoof at the trolley. 'Is that the last of it?'

BB tapped one long talon on the top crate. 'Indeed. That's everything. Once these are loaded up, we're good to go.'

———

Half an hour later, we were loading the same crates into our cargo bay when Bexley dropped what she was doing. 'Oh, oh, oh! It's my dad calling.' She squealed and danced in circles around the room. 'Not the one who owns the company that makes the engines. And not the one with the pink mane. And not the one who's always after me to – well, whatever. Anyways, this is the one I talk about most. Remember I suggested we should all go visit her and her spouses after the next job? She's the one I spent most of my time with growing up. You're really going to like her. Oh, and her spouses are amazing, too. I mean, I don't know the newest one all that well...'

'You should probably answer the call, Bex.' I covered my chuckle with one hand. 'Or she's going to hang up.'

'Oh, right.' Bexley pressed a few buttons.

'Hello? Bexley, is that you?' A new voice spoke into the room.

'Hang on.' Bexley fumbled with her tablet. 'I'm just putting you on the holo.'

'No, Bexley,' replied the voice. 'I think this might—'

'It's okay. It's okay. I've got this.' Bexley was clicking and tapping on the tablet. 'Just ... one ... more... There!' With her final swiping motion, three tiny people burst into existence in the air above her tablet. That is, they probably weren't actually tiny. But they were tablet-sized at the moment. And they appeared to be crowded into a phone booth or maybe a shower.

'No, Bexley,' said a bright white areion with a pearlescent mane and a charcoal nose, who I immediately dubbed Storm in my mind. 'This maybe isn't the best time for you to have all your... No, actually, you know what?' She fiddled with something that looked a bit like a fidget spinner – though one designed for areion hooves instead of human hands. 'We're going to need to impose on your friends, so maybe it is for the best. I mean, it's hardly the ideal way to meet them, but—'

Another areion, this one shorter, plump, and grey with a long purple mane, put her hoof on the first person's arm. 'Sweetheart. It's going to be okay.' She waved cheerfully at all of us. 'Hey, Bexley. Hello, Bexley's friends.'

I waved back. 'Hi, Bexley's family.'

'Oh, everyone. This is my family. Well, one of my families.' Bexley waved a hoof at the holographic representations on top of her device. 'This is my dad.' She pointed to the white areion before gesturing towards the grey one. 'And this is one of my dad's spouses. They've been together since I was a kid. I spent a lot of my adolescence with them after ... well, after things happened.'

The whole introductions with no names thing took some getting used to. Universal translators didn't do names because, apparently, they didn't translate. Sometimes they were a collection of noises another species couldn't make or couldn't hear. Other times they had meanings that were sort of like inside jokes shared by a whole culture or planet. So the universal translator didn't try. Instead, you were meant to assign names of your own choosing to everyone you met. Or let your AI choose for you.

Hence, people introduced themselves and one another using job titles or by describing how they were connected.

Sometimes names came to me easily ... and sometimes they didn't. After naming Bexley's dad Storm in a heartbeat, I called her grey spouse Jean.

But I drew a blank when Bexley got to the one remaining person. 'And this is Storm and Jean's newest spouse. Well, I say newest. They've actually been married now for...' Bexley gestured towards the tallest member of the family, a navy blue person with a short spiky mane – like a brush or a broom. 'How long has it been since you joined the family? It's got to be at least a few years. I remember you were all courting when I moved away to college. I mean, the first college. Or was it...'

When I couldn't think of names, I stuck to an alphabetical naming scheme. The next letter up was P.

Peggy. I decided to call this new step-parent Peggy.

'I'm not sure your friends are all that interested in our family history.' Jean arched an eyebrow as she looked down at Bexley. I hadn't noticed their species even had eyebrows until that moment. 'I'll tell you what, though. I've got a new joke for you. What's purple and makes an annoying sound?'

'Ooh, I know this one,' said Bexley, tapping the side of her head. 'I know it. It's something to do with the smell of the ocean, and the season of the moon, and —'

'Bexley, stop! This isn't a social call.' Storm crossed her arms over her chest. 'Well, no, that is, it is. But also it isn't. There's something we need to talk to you about. It's urgent.'

Aurora began floating back towards the door. 'Come on, everyone. Let's give the family some privacy.'

Storm and Peggy both tilted their heads.

Jean still had one hoof on Storm's arm. 'No.' With her other arm, she pulled Peggy into the embrace. 'This concerns all of you. You should stay.'

I watched Storm's muscles rippling beneath her fur as she clenched. 'This is a secret matter. That's why we're in the... We need to —'

Jean stroked both Peggy and Storm's arms. 'That's true. But we need their help. All of them.'

Storm leant her head on Jean's shoulder. 'They are Bexley's family after all.'

'What is it?' Bexley's pointed ears were swivelling back and forth like little satellite dishes trying to catch a signal. I reached across the space between us and took her hoof in my hand.

Jean took a quick breath. 'There's no easy way to say this.' She clasped her spouses' hooves in her own. 'We're expecting a baby.'

Bexley leapt up off the floor. 'That's amazing! Congratulations. I'm going to have a little semi-sibling. That's the best news I've had all... Hang on.' She chewed the air for a few moments. 'Why do you need our help? Oh, is it a medical problem? Do you mean BB's help? Because BB's an amazing doctor.' She scrunched up her face. 'But I'm sure there are plenty of great doctors on Hwin. Why would you need—'

'Bexley!' Storm held her hooves in front of herself.

'Do you want to maybe let us tell you?' Jean picked up a bowl from somewhere out of the holo-camera's range and tossed a small purple orb into her mouth.

Bexley stopped moving. 'Okay. Sorry.'

Jean was clearly the dedicated spokesperson for the family. 'The embryo is almost ready for transfer to Storm. The surrogate had her scan and—'

Bexley's eyes went wide. 'Oh.'

'Yes, oh.' The mini Jean looked straight into Bexley's full-size eyes. 'She has the defect.'

Bexley sat down on the floor and leant against my leg. 'So...' I dropped down next to her.

Storm stamped her foot. 'We're not doing it.'

BB took a step closer to Bexley and her family.

Peggy blew air out noisily, making Jean's mane flutter.

Jean's muscles rippled beneath her grey fur. 'Hell, no. We're not doing that to our baby.'

Bexley scrunched up her long nose. 'You're not correcting the defect?' Her eyes shot open wide. 'Oh, but that means...'

Jean looked around herself like she thought someone might be listening in. 'Yes, it does.'

'We're leaving.' Storm clutched her fidget spinner.

BB brought one of her hands out from under her wings as she stepped up to face Bexley's family. 'Am I to understand your baby has some sort of genetic issue?'

All three areions on the holo-wotsit tapped their hooves in the air. *Yes*.

BB reached up her hand and ran her talons over her beak. 'And there is a procedure available which would correct it? But you're not planning to have it done?'

Jean squared her shoulders. 'That's right.'

Aurora floated to where BB, her spouse, stood. 'May we ask why?'

'Because it's barbaric.' Storm dabbed at a tear. 'There's nothing wrong with our baby – or any of the other babies born with this so-called defect.'

Peggy reached around and stroked Storm's pale silver mane.

'It's a cruel and antiquated custom,' said Jean. 'It shouldn't even be legal. They say the defect is nothing more than an evolutionary throwback. But Peggy's research... Well, you should explain, sweetheart.' She squeezed Peggy's shoulder.

Peggy adjusted her glasses. 'I'm a molecular biologist with expertise in musculoskeletal physiology.' She spoke in a breathy baritone. I'd never actually figured out how Holly assigned voices to people. It seemed to take them from people I'd known on Earth – either personally or from television, film, or podcasts.

'I've done extensive research into the matter. And it all points to the fact that the so-called defect – which is caused by an autosomal dominant allele on gene THX-1138... Well, simply put, there are no concomitant disorders recorded. And, of course, you could say that there are so few people with the defect uncorrected that there may well be increased risk for certain conditions. But while the N is low, it's hardly non-existent.' Peggy paused and looked around. 'I'm sorry – this must all be going right over your heads.'

Speaking of heads, I scratched mine.

BB wasn't built for sitting but she sort of squatted down next to Bexley and leant over the tablet. 'I'm a doctor, so er… While I can't speak for my colleagues, I certainly understood what you said. Can I ask, though, how does the defect present?'

I figured the conversation was about to get far too technical and scientific for my understanding. But I was sure BB would know what to do.

Jean held her hooves out towards BB, tracing two lines in the air. 'Wings.'

BB's feathers bristled. 'Yes, I have wings.' She spread them out a bit – showing off the riot of colours normally hidden beneath. 'What about them?'

Jean held her breath for a moment. 'I'm sorry – I wasn't clear. What I mean is our child has wings.'

Storm sobbed. 'They want us to cut them off.'

Jean crossed her arms over her chest. 'That's not going to happen.'

BB held Jean's gaze. 'I don't understand. Why would you even talk about cutting a baby's wings off?'

Jean chewed the air. 'It's the law.'

Aurora engulfed her spouse within her gaseous form. 'What do you mean it's the law?'

'The law requires our baby to undergo surgery the day she's born,' Jean said softly. 'Her wings will be taken from her.'

Within the confines of the space they occupied, Storm pressed her way to the front of the group. 'That's why we're calling. We need your help. Help me, Bexley – you're our only hope.'

'We need you to – for want of a better phrase – smuggle

us off this planet.' Jean held her hooves out towards BB's wings again. 'To save our child.'

Bexley sat up. 'We're a collective. I can't decide for everyone. There'll need to be a vote. I can't just—'

I glanced up at the others. 'Everyone in favour of saving Bexley's family, say "yes". And for the record – yes.'

'Yes,' said BB and Aurora in unison.

Henry extruded something that looked like a corkscrew and whirred it aggressively. 'Cup yes. Bollarding baskets and sweet mother of goat, yes. Let's go already.'

Bexley had tears in her eyes as she looked down at Spock. 'What about you?'

I ran my fingers through Spock's fur. 'What do you say? Should we help Bexley's family?'

'Help Bexley.' Spock pawed at my hands. 'Rub cheeks.'

Bexley looked up at her parents. 'Well, I guess that's it. We'll see you soon. Once we calculate the journey, we'll let you know our arrival time. I suppose we might have to stop for unobtainium to recharge our dilithium…' She waved a hoof in the air, brushing the idea away. 'Whatever. It won't be more than a day or so. We'll keep you posted with our arrival time.'

Storm and her spouses were clutching one another in a tight embrace.

'Thank you.' Jean smiled sadly. 'We can't thank you enough.'

'Hey,' said Bexley. 'You never finished the joke. What's purple and makes an annoying sound?'

Jean grinned broadly. 'A salad plate.'

Bexley groaned. 'A salad…' She groaned even louder. 'Oh, Jean, you are such a pervert and a dork, and I love you so much. See you all soon. Love you all. Bye!'

Jokes don't translate well from one language to another.

But they *really* don't work when you're dealing with a whole other species from a completely separate part of the galaxy and no common frames of reference.

Before the call disconnected, Peggy looked at Jean and said, 'A salad plate? I don't get it.'

As Bexley's family blinked out of existence, a strange hush descended on the cargo bay.

BB stood stock still. Aurora made soothing noises and enveloped her spouse. Henry didn't unswear at anyone. She extruded and then retracted various implements. Spock got up and headed for the loo.

Bexley sat on the floor alone. I mean, she wasn't actually alone; she was still sitting next to me. But something about the dejected look on her face told me she felt like she was. I put my arm around her and she collapsed into me.

I held her as the stunned silence continued. I wished I could make this easier on her. A wave of … something … washed over me. Not exactly a chill. Not quite tingles. Not nausea. But not *not* any of those things either.

After a few moments, everyone drifted in and stood before us. Spock returned and joined us on the floor.

'Bexley,' said Aurora gently. 'Are you all right to explain a few things?'

I knew what Bexley needed to tell everyone. She'd confided in me months ago. But I also knew how hard it was opening up to people – even your closest friends. My scalp prickled at the thought of making myself vulnerable. I was pretty sure Bexley felt the same.

Bexley flicked her head, tossing her mane back over her shoulders. 'Yeah, I suppose. You deserve to know.' The look on her face told me she didn't know where to start.

'The cramped space of the cargo bay isn't the best place to do this,' I suggested. 'Why don't we head up to Ten Backwards? It'll give Bexley a minute to think about what she needs to say and we can all get –'

Bexley put a hoof on my knee. 'Thank you, Lem. That's thoughtful. But if I don't get it all out right now, I'll chicken out.'

While the translator couldn't do jokes, it could manage idioms. Most of the time it was able to convey the meaning behind an idiom. Occasionally, it slipped up, though, and we ended up having conversations based on literal interpretations of a cliché.

I nodded. 'Okay, fair enough.'

'Chicken out of what?' BB stroked her wings protectively. 'Why on Quoth would anyone –'

Aurora glowed red and hot pink. 'Let her speak, dear.'

'Okay.' Bexley took a deep breath. 'So, the thing is … most areions are what we call skeletypical. That is, our physical forms adhere to certain norms.' She paused for so long I worried she might not go on. 'But some don't. And it's…' She brushed her forelock down over her long, equine nose.

I rubbed her arm. 'It's okay. I promise.'

'Areion society doesn't look kindly on those who are physically different,' she continued. 'Obviously, as my dad and her spouses explained, infants born with wings are euphemistically said to have *the defect*. Some babies – I think it's something like one in twenty-four or thirty – are born with wings.'

BB reached down and plucked a feather from her chest with her beak. 'And they sometimes excise those wings at birth?'

Bexley looked up. 'No.'

BB jerked her head strangely. 'But I thought you said…'

'They don't remove the wings in *some* cases,' Bexley said. 'They *always* do.'

BB squawked. 'They what? Without waiting to see if they're viable? Without the child's consent?'

Bexley tapped her hooves in the air. 'It's standard practice. In fact, it's the law. And that's not all. Wings can be detected before an embryo becomes a foetus. They deal with those before the baby even learns about them. But there are other types of skeledivergence.'

She looked up at me, then down at the floor.

I rubbed her back as soothingly as I could. 'No one's going to judge you – I promise.' I swallowed.

Spock lay down and rested her chin on Bexley's lap. 'Bexley okay.'

Bexley placed one hoof on Spock's head and with the other, she grasped my hand. 'Another slightly less common type of skeledivergence is what we call the *disorder*. It affects maybe one in forty-eight.' Her voice was so soft I could barely make out the last two words. She paused for a few heartbeats. 'Some areions develop a horn. It grows on the tops of their heads. The disorder – unicornism, to give it its scientific name – doesn't manifest until puberty. Before that time, it's impossible to detect.'

BB stroked her beak thoughtfully. 'Are these genetic differences correlated with any other symptoms?'

Bexley chuckled. It was not a happy sound. 'They say

that unicorns are slow-witted and animalistic. That they're incapable of managing for themselves. If your child grows a horn, you're supposed to check her into a specially built institution.'

Aurora faded into almost invisibility. 'For how long?'

'For life,' replied Bexley. 'They say unicorns are incapable of independent living.'

'And there's no frogging truth to that, is there?' Henry spoke more gently than I was used to hearing from her.

Bexley looked up. And it hit me: Henry already knew. She'd figured it out somehow.

After a moment, Bexley released a breath. 'I like to think I get by okay.'

Aurora shone red. 'This is why you hide your horn?'

Bexley opened her massive horse jaw then closed it again. Eventually she whispered, 'You knew? You all knew?'

Aurora extended a nebulous nub towards her. 'I knew. I don't know whether BB did – we never discussed it.'

BB smoothed her feathers down. 'Well, I am your doctor.'

Henry extended what appeared to be a hairbrush towards Bexley. 'You think my guacamole code was written yesterday? You just magically found a few buckwheat dilithium crystals every time we found ourselves in a bind? Of course I belting knew. Wasn't any of my cupping business, though – was it?'

Unicorn horns were infused with unobtainium. Bexley routinely filed her horn down. She'd used the shavings to recrystallise our dilithium in a pinch a few times.

Our ship ran on dilithium – or at least, that was how Holly translated whatever the substance actually was. If Holly didn't think I was capable of understanding something, it gave me a load of jabberwocky – often drawn from my knowledge of sci-fi. When our dilithium was depleted, we needed unobtainium – another of Holly's special transla-tions – to recrystallise it.

Bexley looked from one to another of our friends, tears streaming down her chestnut-coloured fur. 'You *all* knew? You've known all along? And you really don't think less of me?'

BB clucked and Aurora sort of shimmered. 'Of course we don't think less of you, dear,' said Aurora. 'Why would we?'

Bexley brushed her forelock down over her nose, covering the stub of her horn. 'Well, like, how slow-witted and hard-of-thinking I am. How I'm, you know, basically an animal. Not a person.'

'Birch crackers! With all due respect,' said Henry, who had no respect for anyone, 'that's the most ridiculous thing you've ever said. And you say a lot of ridiculous things.'

My heart soared. Although I'd had confidence that our friends wouldn't judge, I'd still felt Bexley's fear of revealing her secret.

'The only reason I'm not in one of those facilities is that my dads let me hide my horn.' She tossed her head, making her golden mane ripple. 'In fact, the only reason we were able to get away with it is that we were living off-world at the time. You know how one of my dads owns the company that makes ship engines, right? Anyways, whatever. It started to manifest when I was about twelve.'

She got up and paced around the cargo bay. 'If we'd been on Hwin, we'd never have got away with it. Even if people hadn't spotted the great big animal bone protruding from my face, they definitely would have understood the signs. It's really painful and itchy, and you sweat a lot when it grows in. And you're just *so* hungry all the time. I swear, I ate an entire bale of hay before breakfast every day for months.'

She stopped and stroked her forelock.

'If it had happened when we were at home – our old home, I mean – my dads would have had no choice but to surrender me to one of the comfort resorts – which, by the way, is the worst euphemism in the history of euphemisms. So anyways, instead, they all agreed to give me a chance. To see if I could cope.'

She flicked her head. 'Actually, it was around then that my dads split up. I went with Storm and it wasn't long before she married Jean. And they continued to support me and to see if I could make my own way in the world. And, I mean, I couldn't, right? You've seen me. You all know me. I'd be lost without you.'

I glanced at the others but they looked just as confused as I felt. Scratching my head, I asked, 'Sorry, Bexley… I don't… What do you mean? In what way do you not cope?'

Bexley stopped walking and blew out a noisy breath, almost neighing. 'Aurora has to feed me and tidy up after me. Spock tries to keep me from injuring myself … and then BB patches me up when I've injured myself in spite of Spock's support. And you, Lem, you keep me organised and on t—'

A squeaky nervous laugh escaped my lips. 'You keep the engines running! You got us away from the bunnyboos.'

'We're a collective. A community. A *family*.' Aurora shone a mix of hot pink and pale blue. 'Feeding you – all of you – is my job. We all work together. By co-operating, we make all our lives easier.'

BB bobbed her head. 'You understand our lifestyle doesn't represent a failure on your part – on any of our parts, yes? Because it doesn't.'

Bexley resumed pacing. 'But I'm not sure I could even do it all on my own.'

I crossed the room and reached out to her. 'Who says you have to?'

She wrapped her arms around my waist and leant into me. 'I love you. All of you.'

BB picked up her mug from the table and drummed a talon against it. 'Now about these wings…'

Bexley tapped her hooves in the air. 'We need to plan our journey and get underway. I'm pretty sure we'll have to stop for supplies. And I need to process things, I think. Let's reconvene in…' Her voice trailed off as she checked her pendant.

'I've already altered our course,' said Henry. 'There's a space station not far from here. We can load up there. We should arrive in just over an hour.'

While she spoke, I pulled out my phone and started a new email. 'I'm just messaging Megaboulder's team about the job. Blah blah thank you for the opportunity, but unfortunately blah blah unable to take you up on it at this time.'

I hit send and looked up. 'It'll take time to refuel and restock. Why don't we talk over lunch on the station? I'm sure they'll have a pub or a diner or something.'

————

The little space station was drab and dingy. To be fair, though, most space stations seemed drab and dingy after spending a few weeks on one populated by kobolds. The kobolds loved bright colours and good lighting. And they knew how to throw a party.

Bexley, Aurora, and BB walked over to where I stood with Spock and Henry.

BB lifted her wings. 'They said it would take about an hour to get our order together.'

Bexley kicked the floor. 'I asked them to expedite it –

even offered to pay extra. We need to get going. I want to get to my dads as soon as possible.'

Spock ran up and pressed her nose into one of Bexley's hooves. 'Bexley okay.' It wasn't a question – more of a command.

Bexley patted Spock's head. 'I know – I just feel so helpless right now. Like, I should be doing something.'

I put my arm around her. 'Come on. Let's get some lunch.'

We all headed for the station's lone drinking and eating establishment. After taking our seats, we placed our orders. Aurora picked something for Bexley, who wasn't really up to making decisions.

BB stroked the feathers under her beak with her talons. 'Now, about these babies with wings…' Her facial expressions were hard for me to interpret but I was pretty sure she was absolutely seething.

Bexley took a deep breath. 'Okay, like, we were always taught that the wings were a health hazard. That if you didn't remove them they'd cause all kinds of infections and pain and various whatevers. But I guess there's not as much truth to that as they said. I don't know. Peggy's a really good scientist. I trust her. If she says it's all garbage, then I believe her.'

I tried to position myself so I was in Bexley's line of sight, to catch her eye. 'And we already know that what they said about unicorns was wrong. Don't we?'

Bexley shrugged – a human gesture she'd picked up from me. 'I mean, I know I've managed better than they said I would.' She flopped her head down, the tips of her mane landing in her mug of hot apple juice.

I thumped on the table, startling Spock. 'Bexley, no. I call BS. I'm not listening to this.'

'My dear, you've internalised so much ableism that you've persuaded yourself you're less than you are,' said Aurora.

'You're an amazing person. Could you get by without help? I honestly have no idea. But it doesn't matter.'

BB clucked. 'It doesn't mean you deserve to be locked away in some kind of prison. No one deserves that. If you need more support than the average member of your species – and I'm not saying you do – but if you did, then why not take the support?'

'For a meat-based person,' said Henry, 'your blinking CPU functions at a reasonable capacity.' That was probably the highest compliment Henry was capable of giving.

Bexley sat back up and looked around. 'Honestly, sometimes I think it was all a pack of lies and there's nothing wrong with me and I'm happy to be who I am. But then other times I think about how easily I get distracted and like I … I don't know. I don't know what to think.'

She slumped down in her seat and refused to engage any further.

In as much as anyone can know what someone else's pain felt like, I was confident I knew what she was going through. I wished I could make her see her as I saw her. But I couldn't. And I didn't think it would help to keep repeating the same words over and over.

My mouth felt dry. The best thing we could do right then was give her space to process.

———

My stomach flip-flopped as I looked out the window at the planet. Hwin, Bexley's home world. 'No way am I riding that thing.'

Bexley was sitting on the upholstered bench in the mess hall's window. She looked outwards and then back at me. 'The orbital station? What's so scary about an orbital station? And how would you even go about riding one anyways?'

I scrunched my face up. 'Not the station. That!' I waved a hand at the line connecting the station with the planet beneath. 'No way in hell.'

She looked at the planet and back at me yet again. 'What? Do you mean the beanstalk? Why won't you ride a beanstalk?'

As we closed in on the station, I could make out a vehicle of some sort speeding up the pole. My tummy leapt into my throat.

'You'll ride in a transporter pod – but you draw the line at a beanstalk?' Bexley tilted her head to one side with a little grin. 'Are all humans as weird as you?'

'Yes, no, maybe.' I shook my head. 'I don't know. I just… That does *not* look safe. How can that be safe?' I put my hand on Spock's head.

She looked up at me. 'Spock protect.' I gave her a good pat.

The door from the kitchen slid open, admitting Aurora and BB. BB lifted her wings. 'Are you ready for this, Bexley?'

'Almost.' Bexley reached into the holster she wore around her waist. She pulled out a scrap of orange fabric and tied it around her head. 'There we go. That's better.'

Aurora's rainbow hues shifted to a combo of red and royal blue – which struck me as an odd pairing – colours I didn't think I often saw together. I was pretty sure the blue indicated amusement or something like that. But red meant sadness or grief, didn't it? 'We've lived with you for more than six months and we've never seen your horn. What makes you think you'll be spotted by a casual observer now?'

Bexley's shoulders fell. 'Away from Hwin, the worst that

can happen is that someone gets a glimpse of my horn and derides me for it. It would be embarrassing – like, I'd probably want to die of shame. But here…' She turned to look out the window again. 'If someone on Hwin discovers what I really am, I'll be sent to a comfort resort. Forever.'

My stomach churned and I thought I might be sick. Silence fell like a heavy weight. Aurora extended herself to sort of reassuringly envelop Bexley's arm.

I joined Bexley in watching the approaching station. 'How long has it been since you were last home?' I tried not to think about how long it had been for me. What was Devon, my childhood best friend, doing? She moved to Scotland a couple of years before I moved to Canada. Was she still there? Was she happy?

I forced my mind back to the present. Back to Bexley and her reality. This wasn't the time for me to get lost in my nostalgia; today was about Bexley and her family.

Bexley leant into me. 'I haven't lived on Hwin since I was a kid. When I lived with Storm and Jean it wasn't here. We moved around a bit. We stayed on Trantor for a year or so.' She nodded at BB. 'Even spent a few months on Quoth. We lived on a few different space stations – one big, some tiny. I've made a few visits back to Hwin in the last two decades. To visit my other dads, I mean. And my siblings. Well, one of my siblings. The longest I've stayed at any one time was around three months.'

The station filled the window now. 'It'll be okay, you know,' I said. 'We'll get Storm, Jean, and Peggy. You'll be safely away from this place. No one can hurt them or the baby … or you.'

BB pulled Bexley into a hug. 'You never have to come back here ever again if you don't want to.'

The blue had faded – Aurora was almost entirely red now.

'If the other members of your family want to see you, they'll come to you.'

There was a soft thud as we docked with the station.

'But it's my home,' whispered Bexley.

My throat tightened. 'You can come back – you just don't have to.' I stroked Bexley's arm. 'Are you ready?'

She chewed the air for a moment. 'Yeah, let's get this over with.'

## 3 / LEM AND THE BEANSTALK

Even though the thought of it made my stomach flip-flop, we all queued up for a trip down the beanstalk. Almost all the people around us were areions. Most planets we'd visited were populated by many different species. It made me realise that Bexley was the only areion I'd ever met. I wondered if they were a bit isolationist. Obviously they were members of the GU, so they must not be completely cut off from the rest of the galaxy. But we did get more stares than usual.

Surrounded by so many areions, I put a hand on my chest to steady my breathing. Don't get me wrong – I love Bexley, but the first time we met I went into anaphylactic shock. The antihistamines BB made for me were far more effective than any I'd ever used on Earth – but just being surrounded by so many people who could kill me by accident made me nervous.

My fear of the beanstalk and my anxiety about being surrounded by so many areions multiplied one another, leaving me in a state of near panic. I could feel my heart pounding a rhythm in my chest.

'You're sure—' My voice cracked. It was like going

through puberty all over again. 'You're sure this thing is safe?' I pressed my face against the glass and tried to look down the length of the beanstalk. It disappeared into the clouds. 'Can't we take the transporter pods instead?'

'Space elevator technology is much older than transporter pods,' said BB.

I scrunched up my face. 'Not really selling it to me here, Doc.' Deep breath. I counted primes to still my mind. *Two, three, five, seven, eleven, thirteen.*

Aurora glided closer. 'What my lovely spouse means is that the technology has been used and refined for thousands of years.'

'This beanstalk's been in use for more than seventy years.' Bexley moved to position herself in front of me. 'Before that, back in my grandparents' day, people had to launch a rocket every time they wanted to leave the planet. It was incredibly inefficient and laborious. Interestingly, though, that's how my dad's engine company started. They made the best getoff engines around.'

I spun to face Bexley. 'I thought getoffs ran on transporter technology.' Distraction was good. Focus on something else.

'Oh, sure. These days they do but back then—'

'Stand back for arrival!' shouted the areion whose job it was to oversee the queue. She stalked the length of the platform, making sure everyone was where they were supposed to be.

With an enormous and terrifying sound, a pod like the ones on the London Eye zoomed into existence from below us. I stumbled backwards, landing on my arse, and knocking into a party of areions behind us.

'Put your tree on a leash,' shouted a person with blueish-grey fur and a charcoal mane.

'I'm sorry.' What kind of mess had I caused? How humiliating.

Bexley took two steps towards the shouty person, who was significantly taller than she was, and opened her mouth to reply. But, before she could say anything, the attendant rushed over. 'I'm sorry, customer, but this person is correct. If you can't restrain your beasts and your ... animated plant at all times, they'll have to be restrained.' She looked our party up and down. 'In fact, I'm not convinced you can handle these beasts on your own. Come with me, please.'

The door to the pod – the bean, I guess – opened and areions of all shapes, sizes, and colours spilt out around us.

BB squawked. 'What beasts? What are you talking about?'

Spock stepped out from behind Bexley. The attendant looked at her. 'Ah, there are two of you. That's something, at least. Please follow me.' She held up a hoof, indicating we should head that way.

Bexley stamped her hoof. 'No. These are my friends. They are people, not beasts. And definitely not animatronic trees. How dare you?'

'Customer, please. I'm sure we can sort this out.'

'I should apologise to the person I landed on.' I looked around to see if I could spot her, but the streams of people flowing around us had become more of a tidal wave.

'Perhaps we should do as the attendant asked,' said Aurora. 'I'm sure we can explain everything and get back on track.'

'Please,' said the attendant. 'Listen to ... whatever ... whoever said that.'

Muscles along Bexley's shoulders stood out in stark relief. 'Fine. Let's get this over with. What's one more humiliation?'

The attendant led us to the end of the platform, where she

had a small office-cum-meeting space. The key word being *small*. The six of us plus the attendant barely fit into the room.

She pressed a button on her pendant and then spoke into it softly. After a few moments, she looked back up at us. 'The manager will be with you shortly. Thank you for riding the beanstalk today.' With that, she left us locked in the too-small room.

'We haven't ridden the beanstalk yet today, you massive jerkhole,' Bexley shouted at the closed door.

I fought the desire to put my hands on my hips as doing so would mean elbowing at least two of my friends. 'Now what?'

'I don't know, sandwich. Have you tried not sitting on random honking strangers? That might have been a nice place to start.' Henry jabbed some kind of implement I couldn't see into the back of my thigh.

'Ow, you prig.' I swatted the implement away – or at least tried to. 'I didn't sit on her. I fell on her.'

'Oh.' Bexley drew the word out several beats. 'That makes so much more sense then. I wondered why you did that.'

———

'This is humiliating,' I said as we boarded the bean an hour later. A half-dozen or so areions were already waiting.

'But you often tie yourself to Spock in this way,' said BB. 'Is it humiliating because you're tied to Bexley this time?'

I scowled as I tried not to look out the window. We had to be several kilometres above the planet Hwin. 'At least you persuaded them you were a person, Doc.'

'Yes, although I suspect they think I'm actually the GU

President.' BB shook her feathers out indignantly. The Galactic Union was basically the space version of the EU. It was a supraplanetary body whose main purposes were facilitating trade and upholding person rights. Individual member planets retained their sovereignty but they committed to working together for the advancement of all.

'You did show them a picture of the President, though,' said Bexley.

BB squawked and fluttered her wings. 'I was trying to make them see that the peri are one of the most highly regarded species in the GU!'

When the bean began its descent, I got that same feeling I always got in lifts aboard ships or space stations: I could tell we were moving but not in which direction. Something about artificial gravity and nullification fields. *Whatever. I know project management – not space mechanics.*

'Hey, at least none of them put bollarding rubbish on your head,' said Henry as she removed yet another discarded cup from atop herself. She rolled over to the bean's actual bin and placed the cup inside.

We must've passed into the planet's gravity field at that point as I realised I actually felt like we were moving downwards. And much too fast for my comfort, at that.

Bexley headed to the outer edge of the bean. So she could get a better look at our impending doom, I guess. The leash around my waist yanked me after her. The clouds raced towards us at shocking speed. I grabbed the bar so I didn't accidentally fall and cause another interspecies incident.

She fingered Spock's harness. 'This isn't bad, actually. I might get one made with pockets and carabiners. Then we'll be blanket-armour twins.'

Since Spock's harness was never going to fit me, the best way to leash myself to Bexley had been for her to wear it.

The lead clipped to her chest and then formed a belt around my waist. Looking at her sceptically, I stood as far from her – and more importantly the window – as the leash would let me.

She tossed her mane back over her shoulder. 'Oh, I don't mean we need to be tied to one another all the time. Just the harness itself. It's comfy and utilitarian. I'm starting to see why you wear one.'

I glanced down at my hoodie, mini-skirt, and leggings. Hardly what I'd call a harness. But then I'd never managed to successfully explain the concept of clothing to my friends. The closest I'd ever got was 'blanket-armour', which seemed at least vaguely accurate. Pockets, though. Pockets everyone understood. 'How are you holding up? Is it tough being back?'

Bexley nickered awkwardly. 'Yeah, no, for sure. It is and it isn't, you know?'

Moments later, we emerged from the cloud layer. The ground raced towards us at an incomprehensible speed. All my muscles strained and I clung to the grab bar like my life depended on it. Which it kind of did. 'Yep.' I understood – I just couldn't speak while I was so busy being terrified.

We continued our plunge to the ground at figurative, if not literal, warp speed. 'We're all going to die,' I screamed.

And then, just like that, we stopped. Everyone was staring at me – my friends and the six other passengers in the bean.

People were muttering. I caught the words 'control' and 'cactus' and 'tree' several times.

My face burning, I turned to look out the window. We weren't yet on the ground. In fact, we hadn't even stopped moving. But now we were floating downwards at a leisurely pace – not the frenetic race to the surface that I had been so sure was going to kill us.

The city was beautiful but utterly alien. I mean, I guess all worlds other than Earth were alien to me. But Hwin seemed more so than any of the others I'd visited. I wasn't even sure what I was looking at. It had to be a city – but I couldn't tell the buildings from the plant life. If there even was plant life. Most planets had clearly delineated buildings and thorough-fares. Even if the foliage wasn't green, it was usually easy to identify. Not here.

After a few more moments, we slid to a graceful, totally un-scary stop. An attendant pulled the door open and urged us all to exit quickly. She pointed at Bexley. 'And you … keep your animatronic cactus under control.'

———

'Today's the day of the transfer procedure,' said Bexley as she set off from the beanstalk platform.

We all trailed after her as she ran through the … I wasn't sure whether it was a concourse or a street. Were we inside or outside? I couldn't tell. It kind of reminded me of the Canary Wharf DLR station in that it seemed to be partially covered but not entirely enclosed. 'I told Jean we'd meet them at the clinic.'

'Please slow down.' BB was huffing and panting. 'This gravity is very hard on me. My bones were not made for this.'

I hadn't noticed the increased weight – at least, not consciously. But it explained why my breathing was laboured and I felt like I needed a long nap. Bexley paused to let us catch up. The moment we did, she set off again.

The areions we encountered ranged in size and hue. Some

were solid-colour, like Bexley. But others were patterned like leopards or zebras.

'I'm very curious about your reproductive processes,' said BB as we hustled to keep up with Bexley even at her new, slower pace. 'What is this transfer?'

A travellator ran down the middle of the thoroughfare. It was fenced off; presumably, you could only board at designated spots. The slidewalk itself was striped in varying degrees of skin tones – well, human skin tones. I wondered what those colours meant to areions.

Bexley stopped suddenly and turned to face the rest of us. 'Okay, so you know how when an embryo is ready to become a foetus, it moves from the egger-parent to the pouchy-parent for deuteration, right?'

I knew *most* of those words, or at least thought I did. But putting them together in that order made no sense to me. I looked around but the city was equally confusing. To our right was a display of what appeared to be oversized human hands in various poses.

BB shook her feathers. 'I see! So you're exomarsupials?'

Someone dropped a bag on Henry's lid.

Bexley grimaced. 'Yeah, no, sorry. Not exactly. I mean, sort of. It's hard to explain.'

A tall grey areion approached our group. She wore a large official-looking pendant on a lanyard around her neck. 'Good day, citizen. I'm going to have to ask you to put your beasts and animated trees in crates or at least on leads.'

BB squawked. 'For pity's sake! I am not a beast. I am a highly skilled doctor. I trained on Quoth, specialising in interspecies medicine. I've worked on fourteen planets and treated patients from thirty-seven different species.'

*Why did everyone keep calling me a tree?*

Bexley squared her shoulders, pushing her chest out.

'These people are neither beasts nor cacti; they are my friends.'

'Not again,' I muttered.

The cop did a double-take as she faced me with eyes wide. 'Sorry, sorry,' she muttered before scuttling off.

Bexley led us through an opening in the slidewalk barrier. Close up, I noticed it moved in sections. The outer strip – a pale ivory – moved at a crawl. As you got closer to the centre, the stripes got progressively darker and the speed increased. The second one was a pinkish porcelain, matching my skin. The fast lane in the centre was a deep umber.

Before stepping onto the slidewalk, Bexley turned to face the group. 'Everyone's used one of these before, right? No one's going to fall? Henry, there's no lip, so you should be able to roll right on – if you're comfortable with it.'

'Well, thank pluck for small mercies,' said Henry. Some of the places we'd visited had been surprisingly – or perhaps unsurprisingly – inaccessible to people on wheels.

Bexley tapped her hooves. 'Good. Lem, how about you? Do you want to hold my hoof?'

I sighed. 'Yeah. Probably for the best.'

I managed to board without making a tit of myself. I hadn't noticed before, but the slidewalk had grab bars at various intervals. BB climbed atop one, using it as a perch. The others seemed fine without them – even Henry, who I worried might roll off the edge by accident the next time we passed an entrance.

'The clinic's a few kilometres from here,' said Bexley as we settled into the fast lane. 'It's mainly this line all the way there. Once we get off, we can take a second short ride or we can walk the rest of the way.'

I spied a larger set of the hand statues I'd seen before. Most were in a sort of cupped pose – but a few were making fists or waving. I saw at least one in a Vulcan salute. They occupied a large open space with some sort of beige rock floor.

After prying one of my hands from the grab bar, I tapped Bexley on the shoulder. 'What are those?'

Bexley followed the line of my arm and then looked back at me. 'Do you not have parks where you come from?'

I scrunched my face up. 'Yeah, we have parks. But I mean, what's with all the hands?'

Bexley chewed the air for a few seconds. 'What hooves?'

Holding the grab bar one-handedly again, I held my hand out in the same baseball-catching pose as most of the statues or whatever they were. 'The hands.'

Bexley's head whipped over to look at the park again, her long blond mane flying as she did so. After a few seconds, she turned back, her jaw hanging slack. 'Your hooves ... they look like little cactus-trees. How weird is that? I wonder why I never noticed before. Holy crap! That's so bizarre. Even your skin looks like the cladode of a tree. How come you never mentioned that?'

My mind reeled. 'What?'

She tapped her hooves on the grab bar. 'Is it weird for you to eat nutrient porridge?'

'What?' As so often happened, I felt lost in this conversation. Twisting herself around on her grab bar-cum-perch, BB bent down to face us. 'Lem, have you noticed how much you resemble the local flora?'

'Oh, this is our stop.' Bexley started making her way across the slower lanes – the opposite direction from the side we'd entered on. I stumbled as I tried to keep up with her but I managed to avoid landing on – or even touching – anyone.

We all agreed to walk the rest of the way to the clinic. It gave me a chance to look around a bit more. The buildings were brightly coloured and looked more like rock formations than anything – at least to my eye. There was an abundance of plant life – it just took me a while to recognise it as such. What I'd thought was a rock floor in the first park was actually a sort of moss-like substance. It came in varying shades of beige and brown.

I reached out to touch one of the hand-trees – but Bexley stopped me, my hand was mere centimetres from its surface. 'Careful. You're fragile.'

'What?' For a while, that one word seemed to be all I had to contribute to most conversations. I thought I'd got past that phase of my life in space. It seemed not.

Bexley used her hoof to indicate the fine hairs that covered the hand. 'The little spikes – they might cut your skin.'

'Huh?' – which wasn't really an improvement on my previous utterance.

The blue tarmac was smooth and level. This thoroughfare was that same sort-of-inside, sort-of-outside space as the one at the base of the beanstalk. There didn't seem to be any vehicles anywhere. Occasionally, someone pulled or pushed a cart or baby buggy. A few people used what I could only assume were wheelchairs or mobility scooters. But for the most part, people walked. At least, the ones not riding the slidewalks did.

Bexley led us to a green building. Well, it looked more like a hill than a building. Apparently it was the maternity clinic. Maternity wasn't the right word given how different the areion reproductive system was – but it was the closest one I had. Maybe fertility clinic would be better.

When we ·tried to enter the building, someone who I assumed was a security guard ran over, waving her arms in a pretty clear gesture. 'No! No animals – or whatever *that* is. Get them out of here.'

Aurora floated to the front of the group. Her dominant colour was pale green – one I'd never noticed in her before. 'Greetings, worker. I assure you, my friends and I are not beasts. We are beings from disparate worlds, who have been invited to join some friends of ours on their joyous occasion.'

The security guard sniffed at us, then looked to Bexley. 'Is this true?'

'Yeah, my dad is Storm. She and her two spouses are here for an embryo transfer.'

The security guard leant close to me. 'How'd you get it to move?'

Spock positioned herself in front of me and growled.

'All right, friend.' The security guard raised her hooves while looking at Spock. 'No need to get shirty with me.' She turned to Bexley. 'Wait right here. Do not allow any of them to attempt to come further into the building.' She pointed at us, then approached the front desk.

'We're clearly causing these people distress,' I said. 'Or at least I am. Maybe we should go somewhere and wait.'

BB clicked her beak. 'Well, I for one want to learn about the reproductive processes. I'm presumably going to serve as med—'

Aurora noisily cleared her throat. Not that she had a throat. Whatever. She made a noise to cover BB's words and to prevent her from giving even part of our plan away.

A new areion approached us. She was mottled blue with an obsidian mane. The most unexpected thing about her was that she was wearing what appeared to be a mask – on her crotch. 'Good morning. I understand you've been invited by Storm. It's highly unusual to have off-worlders present for a transition ... but it's fine.' She smiled warmly and gestured for us to head into the building proper.

The security guard hustled over. 'You can't – it's unsanitary.'

'Thank you, guard. That will be all,' said our guide.

She led us through a series of corridors and up several ramps. I noticed that although the space was divided into sections using curved glass walls, there weren't any rooms as such. And definitely no doors. We passed families and procedures I couldn't begin to understand. Though no one seemed to object, our presence felt intrusive and wrong. After a few minutes, we were ushered to a space with three familiar faces.

Storm snoozed on a sort of chair-bed. Her mouth was

open and her breathing was slow and steady. Various leads and tubes connected her to pieces of equipment.

Jean – who was shorter than Bexley and twice as wide – ran and embraced her step-child. 'Bexley! Bexley's friends. Hello, hello. Welcome. We're so glad you could join us. Thank you for coming.' Up close, her grey fur was softly striped in a subtle monochrome.

Peggy came over and put her arm around Jean, who still clung to Bexley. She was nearly as tall as I was. Her short spiky mane was a sort of steel blue. I wondered if wearing it short was a stylistic choice or if it indicated something. Then again, maybe that was the way it grew. 'The procedure just finished. Storm will be monitored closely until she wakes up to ensure the foetus takes hold properly.'

Jean leant into Peggy. 'Storm should sleep soundly for about a day. We'll bring you all back to the house so we can rest and eat. But first, the surgeon's supposed to stop by for a chat. Please make yourselves comfortable here – it should only be a few minutes.'

Bexley nuzzled Jean and then did the same to Peggy. 'No worries. We'll be fine.'

'I'd like to speak to one of the medics as well,' said BB. 'I want to understand your anatomy better – especially if I'm to be treating a gestating areion in the coming weeks.'

Jean reached a hoof towards BB. 'Please, you mustn't give anything away,' she whispered, glancing around furtively. 'If anyone suspects anything, we will be arrested. *Please.*'

Bexley's throat bobbed as she swallowed. 'Jean's right. Off-worlders are pretty rare on Hwin – even in a big city like this one. People will remember you.'

BB looked shaken. 'I'm sorry. This gravity is exhausting me – I must not be thinking clearly. You're right. It's professional curiosity – but I completely understand the need for discretion.'

Peggy tapped her hooves in the air. 'I understand, believe me. Curiosity is what drives my research. But if anyone's suspicions are aroused, you'd definitely be rem —'

A plump mauve areion waddled into view. 'Greetings. Hope I'm not interrupting anything. Oh my! Quite the group we've got here. I say – are you a velarian?' This was directed to Aurora.

Bexley and I glanced at one another. It looked like we'd got away with that. But we'd have to be more careful in future.

Aurora floated over to the newcomer. 'I am indeed. Well spotted, er…'

'Surgeon,' the areion finished.

'Well spotted, Surgeon. I am, as you say a velarian. And this is my spouse, a peri who is also a doctor.' Aurora pointed to BB with a gaseous nub of an appendage. 'And these are our friends, a lonely robot, a dog, and a human. Oh, and Storm's adult offspring, of course.'

The surgeon approached me cautiously. 'Marvellous. How fascinating. You look so much like a tree.' Her nostrils flared as she sniffed the air. She held a hoof up towards me. 'May I touch your skin? Anywhere that you choose, of course. I've just never encountered anyone like you. You're a rare treasure.' I wasn't sensing any aggression from her – only curiosity.

Most people we had met viewed me as a freak – not because I was trans but rather because humans were so unlike any other species. I held out a hand. 'Thank you for asking, Doctor. Yes, you may.'

'I promise not to hurt you.' Gently, she took my arm by the sleeve and peered at my hand. 'Well, that is, I promise to *try* not to hurt you. Please let me know if I do by mistake. You even have the fine spikes like trees. Well, like our cactus-trees do. I imagine the flora looks quite different where you're from, hey?'

I smiled – I didn't know why but I liked her. 'They do indeed.'

'Those aren't spikes on her arm,' said Bexley. 'It's fur. Touch them – they're soft.'

Areions had retractable thumbs in their hooves. The surgeon extended one and used it to touch the fine hairs on my arm carefully. 'Oh my! How unexpected.' She looked up at me. 'Thank you.'

Pressing her hooves together, she continued, this time addressing Bexley's family. 'Good afternoon. My name is [no frame of reference]. I'm the surgeon who'll be doing the procedure on your baby. I just wanted to put your minds at ease and ensure you understand what's involved.'

The hair stood up on the back of my neck. This person who I'd so instinctively liked, who'd been so gentle with me, was the one who wanted to perform totally unnecessary surgery on Bexley's semi-sibling. She intended to cut off an innocent child's healthy wings. My hand rose to my mouth as I struggled to swallow down the bile.

Peggy touched her right hoof to her left shoulder. 'I'm a biochemist. My area of specialism is orthopaedics.'

The surgeon's eyes sparkled. 'Ah, so no questions from you then, I'll bet?' She turned to Jean. 'And you? Anything you'd like to know?'

Jean was a better actor than I expected. She smiled beat-ifically. 'Thank you. I suppose I'm the stereotypical anxious parent. Are there any risks involved?'

The surgeon bobbed her head. 'Well, no procedure is entirely without risk, of course. But this procedure is completely routine. You're standing in the finest fertility care clinic on Hwin. I perform dozens of penna-arthrectomies every year and have done so for decades. It is incredibly rare that we see any side effects at all.'

BB ground her beak. Aurora moved to partially engulf her spouse's shoulder.

Jean tapped the air in front of herself. 'I see. Of course. I told you – I'm just a big old Nervous Nellie. What kind of side effects are we talking about? However infrequent they may be...' She did an anxious little tap-dance.

The surgeon placed a reassuring hoof on Jean's shoulder. 'Your concern for your child tells me you're a good parent. The most common side effect is that the defect grows back. If that happens, then you would need to bring the child back to the hospital – probably a few years from now. We'd go back in and correct things.'

Jean sniffed and tapped her hooves in the air. She buried her face in Peggy's broad chest.

'Well, I should, er, let you all get back to your business. I'll be around if you have any other questions. Storm will probably sleep for another twenty-six hours or so. If that's everything, then I'll see you again in about a month. It was lovely to meet you all.' She touched her hoof to her shoulder and disappeared amongst the warren of patient spaces and hospital equipment.

'I don't think she heard anything,' I whispered to Bexley once the surgeon was gone.

She held out her hands and looked up at me. 'We got lucky. We have to be more careful, though.'

I nodded.

Jean bustled to the bed where Storm still snoozed, hooked up to various machines, and kissed her on the forehead.

Peggy did the same – though I wouldn't describe her movements as bustling. She was too gangly and awkward for that.

'We should go,' said Jean. 'Will you join us for dinner?'

'That's a great suggestion. Thank you,' I said. 'We should go somewhere where we can speak more freely.'

Peggy flicked her head. 'I'm not sure about that – but we'll definitely be comfy there.'

'As much as that sounds like an excellent idea,' said Aurora, 'I believe I need to get my spouse back to the *Teapot*. This gravity is proving too much for her.'

BB was breathing heavily. 'That's probably for the best. I hoped I'd be all right for a few hours at least, but I think I've reached my threshold.'

Jean laid a hoof very carefully on BB's wing. 'Of course. I look forward to getting to know you both better over the coming days. Will you be all right getting back to the beanstalk station on your own?'

'I can guide them.' Henry revved her wheels. 'I'll join the gas bag and the feather duster. You know, since the idea of stuffing myself full of decomposing plant matter has about as much appeal to me as signing up for an off-cycle defrag.'

———

When we stepped outside, it seemed a bit darker than when we'd arrived less than an hour ago. 'So, where to?'

'It's this way.' Jean took Bexley by the arm and headed out to the left, the opposite direction from when we'd arrived. 'We've moved since you last visited, Bexley. You've not seen our new place.'

'I can't wait.' Bexley was practically skipping. 'I've seen

bits of it on our holo-calls. But it's not the same as being there.'

'We're living on a wind farm now.' Jean led us onto another slidewalk.

'Are you? That's so cool,' said Bexley. We made for the centre lane once again. 'I've always thought it would be cool to live on a wind farm. Oh, that reminds me… What did one windmill say to the…' She swished her tail back and forth. 'No, hang on. Two windmills are standing in a field. One says to the other … I think. Wait…'

Jean looked at her step-child with a twinkle in her eye. 'One says to the other, "Where do you get off?"'

'And it says, "I don't".' Bexley clapped her hooves together. 'I love that one.'

The pair of them laughed uproariously. Even a couple of people nearby looked like they were trying not to chuckle.

Peggy pushed her glasses up her long nose. 'Don't worry, Lem. I don't get it either.'

I smiled. 'Thanks, Peggy.' That little admission made me like her more. All around us, the city sprawled out in every direction. The ground was varying shades of beige and brown. There were more of those weird trees here and there – in every size and shade of human skin tone.

But then I spotted something even weirder. Human heads. Just sticking out of the ground. Or in pots. They were sort of featureless: not much of a face to speak of. But they had ears and hair.

Bexley grabbed my arm as she gestured at them. 'Holy crap! I totally forgot about the sacred cabbages. Isn't it cool? You look just like a cabbage.'

Because of course the heads were cabbages.

## 5 / PLEASE STOP SAYING PENIS

After about twenty minutes, we exited the slidewalk. It took me a few moments to realise what had changed: the strange partial dome above us was gone. We were under open sky; the city was thinning out.

Turning to face me and Spock, Jean said, 'It's a couple of kilometres from here. Are you both okay to walk the rest of the way? We do have a farm vehicle – we could get someone to bring it if you'd be more comfortable. I know our gravity is hard on you.'

Spock wagged her tail. 'Walkies?'

'Spock is clearly on board and I'll be fine,' I assured her. But I did pull my inhaler from my pocket and take a hit. The difference in gravity was barely perceptible – at least on a conscious level. But it was making everything a little bit more work. Still... 'The walk will be nice.'

Jean tapped her hooves in the air. 'If you're sure ... but please let us know if you change your mind at any point.'

The road ahead stretched out for miles. Hwin must be bigger than Earth because the horizon seemed so much further away. The air smelled spicy: pepper and something like cardamom.

The ground was covered in more of the beige moss. Hand-trees lined both sides of the road. They ranged in height from not quite my waist to probably double my height. The colours varied from ivory to a rich, warm brown. And every last one of them looked exactly like a human hand.

As we passed an especially large hand-tree-cactus-whatever on my left, I gasped. Okay, actually, I shrieked. 'What the hell is that?'

Spock did that awkward half-squat-half-leg-lift thing that girl dogs do as she paused to pee on the … the … the thing.

The whole group stopped walking. Bexley looked at the plant and then back at me with a puzzled look on her face. 'It's an eggplant tree, silly. Did you think all our trees looked like your funny little forked hooves?'

Jean punched Peggy playfully on the shoulder. 'You know everything about Hwin vegetation. Come on, I know you're dying to explain.'

I snapped a few pics before I started walking again. If I ever met another human, they were going to die laughing.

'I certainly don't know everything. Only a bit.' Peggy pushed her glasses up her nose. 'But … er … the ones that resemble Lem's hooves are called asparagaceae. I believe Bexley mentioned that you primarily eat nutrient porridge when you're travelling. It's interesting to note that the root of the asparagaceae is used in producing porridge powder. It provides the majority of the complex carbohydrates.'

The further we walked the more of the *other* trees I saw.

Peggy coughed. 'What's also interesting about the asparagaceae is that, on Hwin, we mainly eat the flesh and the cladode. They're really fascinating plants, actually. In fact, all the plant life on Hwin is similar. The stalks can be harvested

and will regrow in just a few months. Even taking the root –
or rather part of it – doesn't necessarily kill the tree. With a
mature asparagaceae, you can remove up to eighty per cent
of the root and the tree will grow back.'

'That's amazing,' I said nodding my head. 'But what
about the willies?'

All three areions stopped and gawped at me. Bexley
looked at her two step-dads and then at me. 'I'm sorry … the
what? I don't think that translated correctly.'

I felt the heat rise in my cheeks. 'The, er…' I waved a
hand at one of the X-rated cactus-tree-things.

The three areions looked at one another again. And then
back at me.

Bexley sniffed the air. 'The word you used – was it the
reproductive organ of a seeder-sexed person?'

My entire face was burning. 'These trees … they
… er… Well, they look like genitalia. Human genitalia. You
know … during.'

'Do you mean a penis?' Jean asked. 'That's remarkable.
Our penises look quite different from that. Do you want to
see mine?' She reached down – about where her belly button
would be if she were human – and started to pull back
her fur.

My hand shot up. 'No! I do not want to see your penis.'
My face was actually on fire; I was sure of it. I fought back a
sneak attack of the giggles.

They all studied me.

'I assure you,' said Jean, 'there is nothing funny about my
penis. It's quite a nice penis.'

Peggy put her arm around her spouse. 'It's true. I've often
remarked on what an attractive penis it is.'

Bexley studied my face. 'I know you've got some weird
taboos about being disarmoured. But I always thought that

related to the hole you've got in your midsection. Do you have something against penises? Hey, do you have a penis?'

'Can we all please stop saying penis?' I begged. 'It's not that I'm uptight.' I scratched my head. 'Okay, yes. Maybe I am uptight. I suppose I am.' *The hole in my... Wait, did she mean my belly button?*

We stood awkwardly in the middle of the road while I tried to gather my thoughts. Spock took the opportunity to piss on another hand-tree – an asparawotsit.

I sighed. 'Yes, humans, in general, have issues and taboos about their – about our – genitalia. I think almost any human who found herself on your world would feel either embarrassed or amused at those plants. I mean, they look ... so realistic. Like, *so* realistic. With the veins and the head and the skin colour and the scro—' I shuddered. 'It's really quite unnerving.'

I pinched my eyes closed tight for a sec. 'But beyond that, for me, I have ... issues. I don't know if these words are going to even translate for you but...' I let myself count the first six primes in my head while I gathered my courage. 'Bexley, I told you once about the concept of gender. Most people – or, most humans, I mean – have an innate sense of gender. And for most pe— most humans, their gender aligns to the sex they were assigned at birth. And again, most of the time, that matches the observable sex characteristics – a penis or a vagina.'

Deep breath. Or two. 'But not always. Some humans have a gender that doesn't match their assigned sex. And some humans – me, for example – have no innate sense of gender at all. And those humans – both the ones whose gender doesn't match their observable sex and the ones with no gender... Well, we can experience a sense of dysphoria about our bodies. Or even dysmorphia.'

I looked up. 'That was just a string of [no frame of refer-ence], wasn't it?' The last time I'd tried to talk to Bexley about this, we'd discovered that her people had no concept of gender.

Jean bobbed her head. 'There were some rare words in there, to be sure. But I think I understand. You're saying that most people on your world belong to a caste that's somehow related to their physical sex characteristics. But then you talked about people having dysphoria about their sex – and that you are one of those people. Is that correct?'

I weighed up her words in my mind. 'Yeah, that about sums it up.'

'Huh,' said Jean.

Bexley started walking again. 'And so your penis – if indeed you have a penis… Because I'll be honest, I don't actually know if you do. But if you do, then it looks like an eggplant tree. Is that what you're saying?'

The rest of us set out after her. 'I do. And yes. But can we please not talk about it anymore?' My cheeks flushed again. The anticlimax of revealing this bit of truth about myself felt weirdly like setting down a heavy burden only to feel naked without it. I needed a change of subject. 'Also, eggplant trees – really?'

'Oh, yes. Actually, the eggplant tree – or to give it its scientific name, solanum melonphallus – is also a major component in the nutrient porridge.'

I fought back a sudden surge of bile. 'We eat the … the … the phallus things? I've been eating them all along?'

A slight curve in the road brought a host of windmills into view in the distance.

Peggy tapped her hooves in the air. 'Solanum melon-phallus.'

Jean turned back to face Peggy while still walking. 'Most

people call them eggplant trees. Only dorks use the scientific name in casual conversation.'

'Whoa there!' said Bexley with a neighing laugh. 'Did you just call someone else a dork? You are the president of the dorks. You know that, right?'

Jean jiggled her eyebrows. 'Why do you think I married her?'

'Yes, well,' continued Peggy undeterred. 'As I was saying, the eggplant tree is a major component in the nutrient porridge.'

'The roots, you mean?' I swallowed. 'Right?'

'Ah, it's interesting, actually.' Peggy ran a hoof over her short blue mane. 'You're right that when it comes to the asparagaceae—'

'Most people call them plain old asparagus,' said Jean, pausing to plant a kiss on Peggy's nose.

'—it's the root that gets exported for the nutrient porridge and the stalks are eaten here on Hwin. However, with the solanum melonphallus, it's the reverse.'

My throat closed for reasons that had nothing to do with allergies. 'You eat the roots but the, er, shaft is ground up into—'

'Bexley, it's been too long!' Someone came running out of what I had taken to be a blue rocky hill. She was followed by three other adults and a pair of what had to be toddlers running on all fours. 'And you've brought friends. Come in, come in.' She hugged Jean and Peggy at once.

The next letter in my alphabetical naming scheme was Q. I decided to call her Quark.

The children galloped up to me and stared open-mouthed. When I said hello, they squealed and ran away.

'These are our housemates and some of their children,' said Jean. 'Please, come in. We have dinner waiting.'

The house seemed to be shaped a bit like a snail's shell. Rather than an actual door, there was an opening that led into a hall. A couple of metres further on, the interior wall ended, leading us into a wide open space. Instead of windows in the walls, there were skylights in the ceiling. The whole place was bright and airy.

The house gave a new meaning to open-plan living. There was a lounge with sofas and comfy-looking chairs, a large dining area, and at least half a dozen beds. Aside from the four adults and two kids who'd come out to greet us, there were three more people. Judging by the grunted nods we got in greeting, I assumed they were teenagers.

'Please feel free to take off your, er, armour if you'd like.' I saw Quark glance over my shoulder at someone behind me. 'Or not, of course. Your call. I hope you're all hungry. We've got grilled eggplant steaks, mashed asparagus, and wilted hay for dinner.'

Spock was practically drooling on the floor. No, not practically. She *was* drooling. I was starving but my mind was still freaked out over the idea of eating eggplant steaks.

———

When I woke, Bexley and Spock were both snuggled into me. Indeterminate numbers of areions were curled up in big heaps on beds to both the left and right of me.

I got up as quietly as I could, taking care not to jostle Bexley. Spock raised her head and looked at me then flopped back down. I made my way to the bathroom, grateful for the small accommodation of the curtain at the front of the room. They'd put it up just for me. As much as open-plan living worked for this culture, it wasn't to my taste.

There didn't seem to be a lot of shame around the idea of

secrecy. Apparently, you could just say you were going to the secrecy room and everyone accepted it. Whether you went in alone or with others, there was no gossip, no speculation. The bonus for me was that it offered the privacy I needed to get changed.

Once dressed, I wandered around the outer edge of the house, trying hard to stay clear of the sleeping area. I didn't want to wake anyone.

I found Spock in the kitchen with Quark and several of Jean and Peggy's housemates cooking up a storm. Well, Spock wasn't doing any cooking. But she was definitely helping clean up anything that fell.

'Morning.' I raised my hand to my mouth as I stifled a yawn.

'Ah, good morning, human,' said Quark cheerfully. 'Your, er, child has just been telling us how hungry she is.'

No one ever understood my relationship to Spock at first. Or, you know, ever.

I shook my head with a grin. 'I'll bet she did. She'd eat until she made herself sick if I let her.'

'Sounds like one of my kids,' said Quark as she stirred something in a massive pan on the hob. 'Still… Plenty of hungry mouths to feed this morning. I figured you'd probably never had fresh nutrient porridge so I'm making that. We blend it with cauliflower sap and moss berries.'

I refused to imagine what that meant, so I just went with it. 'Is there anything I can do to help?'

She smiled at me warmly. 'Thank you, dear. Why don't you go see if Jean, Peggy, and Bexley are awake yet? Breakfast should be another quarter of an hour. And let them know the hot apple juice will be ready any second now.'

The farewells at the beanstalk base station were restrained and subdued – like everyone was biting their tongues. Bexley and I acted like we were leaving after a short visit with her family. Jean and Peggy had to pretend they weren't going to see us again for many months.

Going back up the beanstalk was possibly even more terrifying than coming down it had been. But eventually, we made it back to the *Teapot*. I was relieved to be home – but we weren't scot-free yet. Or rather, Bexley's parents weren't. Aurora, BB, and Henry were aboard but nowhere to be seen.

We stepped into the lift and directed it down to level zero. Bexley looked up at me, her eyes glassy.

I reached out and took her hoof in my hand. 'It's going to be all right.'

Spock leant into Bexley. 'Be okay, friend Bexley.'

'Thank you, honey.' Bexley chewed her lower lip. 'Is it, though? Even if we succeed, they can never go home again. I suppose I could – but I'd be taking a risk. I mean, well, there's always risk when I go to Hwin.' She reached up and whipped the orange fabric off her head. 'I could be discovered. And then I'd be sent to a comfort resort. But if anyone suspects the real reason for Storm, Jean, and Peggy's disappearance, for me to go to Hwin would endanger them and their baby. Even as it is…'

She trailed off, collapsing into me as the door opened. 'We can't go back – can we?'

I held her, urging her out into the corridor. I understood how she felt – or at least thought I did. Spock and I couldn't go home again either. Part of me missed it. In some ways, Earth still tugged at me. 'Come on. Let's go program the transporter pods. Once we've done that, we can sit and talk.'

She sniffed. 'Okay.'

I rubbed her shoulder. 'I'll make you a hot apple juice and we'll sit in the lounge. Looking at the stars always soothes you.'

She tapped her hooves and picked up the pace. After a few more steps, the door to the transporter room whooshed open. I tapped the control screen to wake it up. 'We want the pods to land in the field behind the house, right?'

Bexley sat down on the floor and threw her arms around Spock. Spock was good at making people feel better. Still clinging to Spock, Bexley replied, 'Yeah, we don't have much choice but to trust their housemates.'

I tapped a few buttons and then zoomed in on the satellite image. Once I was confident I'd picked the right spot, I clicked the button to send three pods. They dropped from their position with a small plopping sound like they were being flushed down a giant toilet.

Bexley took a deep breath. 'It's going to be okay, isn't it?'

'It is.' I nodded and put my arm on her shoulder. 'It'll probably be almost an hour before they get here.' I honestly had no idea whether anything would be okay for Bexley and her family. But I wanted to be strong for her like she always was for me.

We walked down the hall to the kitchen. I removed two mugs from the cupboard and put one in the dispenser.

Spock wagged her tail. 'Feed Spock?'

I gave her a little pet. 'Not now, mate. Sorry.'

As I keyed in the code for Bexley's juice, she stood in the middle of the room, chewing the air.

I handed her the mug. 'Never being able to go back to your home is a big thing – believe me, I know.'

She looked up at me with her eyes wide. 'That's it! At the edge of my mind, I knew you could relate … but I couldn't quite put the pieces together. You and Spock, you're in the same boat – aren't you?'

I took a small canister from one of the cupboards and carefully measured out eighteen grams of orange powder. I shoved the mug into the dispenser and keyed the code for hot water. The mild stimulant was the closest thing I'd found to coffee – and it was nothing like coffee. It tasted more like hot, flowery, Marmite water. And it turned bright purple when the water touched it.

I leant back against the counter and considered Bexley's question while the machine worked. 'I suppose we *could* go home – but I couldn't just slide back into my old life. I've been gone for something like eight months with no explanation. My job is gone. My home is gone. There's almost certainly a police record. Everyone probably thinks I'm dead.'

Running my hand down the length of my ponytail, I continued. 'And I couldn't bring you with me. If you think your people's reaction to me and the others was bad' – I laughed bitterly – 'it's got nothing on what my people would do if they saw any one of you. They'd probably kill you on sight.'

Her mouth fell open. 'Geez, I thought areions were racist. Are your people really that hostile to off-worlders?'

I pulled my mug from the dispenser, the floral aroma filling my nose. 'Come on, let's go through to the mess hall.'

We settled onto the bench seat in front of the window. Spock lay on the floor next to us. I turned the lights down so we could look at the planet below. 'My people don't even believe in life on other planets.'

Bexley snorted hot apple juice out of her nose, spraying it all over the place. 'What – at all? Like, you think you're alone? That you've just got this whole massive universe all to yourselves?'

I looked at Bexley's home world. The sun was beginning to set on the area beneath us. To the left, the planet was in darkness. 'Pretty much.'

She was silent for a while, as she studied the world she might never see again. 'Like, what? Do they not know about … um, you know … everything? Are they unaware of just how much universe there is in the universe? Do they honestly think it all exists only for them? I mean, that's gotta be the most selfish thing I've ever heard. I can't believe someone as awesome as you comes from a place as back-wards as that.'

I rested my head against the window. 'Hey, having seen a little glimpse into how your society views you, I can truly say – right back at you.' I sighed. 'But yeah. I know. When I look back to my life on Earth, I find it uncomfortably hard to believe some of the so-called facts – things I was always told I had to accept.'

Bexley took another sip of her juice. 'Fair. My people

aren't exactly beacons of awesomeness in the galaxy. I'm sorry they treated you so badly.'

I sat bolt upright. 'Me? Bexley, they made me tie a lead around my waist for half an hour and a few people looked at me funny. You're the one they want to institutionalise. Those two things are not remotely the same.'

'The comfort resorts are awful.' Bexley's words were barely a whisper. She pushed her forelock down over her long nose. 'I went to one once. I was just a foal. We were all still together, living with this family who had three kids... Whatever. Anyways, I worshipped this one foster sibling, Drummer.'

I let Holly choose names for people I'd never meet or that I'd only interact with just once.

Bexley continued. 'I followed her everywhere. Styled my mane like her. Listened to the same bands she did. Tried to do everything she did. I thought she was just the epitome of cool, you know?'

I nodded. Although I'd never had siblings, I knew how kids could be.

Bexley leant over and set her empty mug on the floor. 'But, one day, when she was about twelve, Drummer started getting super grumpy. All the time. Then she complained about her face being itchy. I didn't understand why at the time – like, I had zero clue about any of it. All the adults started freaking out and speaking in hushed voices. I didn't know what was happening. Drummer was constantly crying and screaming and clawing at her head. And then she started ... well, there was blood dripping down her nose.'

I was pretty sure I knew what was coming. My heart burned for Bexley. And for Drummer.

She blew out a noisy breath. 'My dads sat me down and explained that Drummer was sick – that she couldn't be cured. That her parents were doing the best thing for her by sending her to a place where she'd be happy and she could feel accepted and supported.'

My stomach was doing backflips just listening to this.

'The whole family went with her to the comfort resort. It was like a whole "show her it's not so bad" party. I tried to put on a brave face. I didn't want Drummer to be unhappy – but it was the worst place I'd ever been.'

Bexley snatched my hand and clung to it. 'The worst. I *cannot* go there. I can't.'

I wrapped my arms around my best friend. I ached for how much this was tearing her up inside. 'I know, sweetie. You won't have to. No one should have to. But we – all of us – won't ever let that happen. No one's taking you anywhere.'

She snorted loudly. 'I remember the worst thing about the comfort resort. You're going to think this is really weird, but for an areion, it's a big deal. The residents had to sleep separately. They had these little prison cells – rooms, I guess. And everyone had to sleep by themselves. It was just so horrible. I'd never seen anything like it. To be honest, I never experienced anything like that until the *Teapot*.'

I leant away from her, holding her at arm's length so I could look her in the eye. 'Wait. You never slept alone until the *Teapot*?'

'Never.'

I frowned. 'Do you like it?'

Bexley held my gaze. 'Do I like sleeping alone?'

I nodded.

'No, of course not. No one does – do they?'

'Some people do, definitely.' I took a sip of my now luke-warm helbru. 'You know you're always welcome to join me and Spock in our room, yeah?'

'For real?' She looked at Spock. 'You wouldn't mind?'

Spock wagged her tail. 'What?'

Bexley stroked Spock's ears. 'You wouldn't mind if I slept in your room with you?'

'Not bedtime,' replied Spock – and then went back to sleep.

'She wouldn't mind, I promise.' I grinned. 'And neither would I.' Then I gazed off at the planet. 'You know, so long as I've got plenty of BB's antihistamines.'

'Yeah, fair. I wouldn't want to accidentally kill you in your sleep.'

I tapped my fists on the window. 'That would not be ideal.'

'I feel like if I'm going to kill you, it should be deliberate.'

I chuckled. 'Seems reasonable. And I'd like to be awake while we're at it.'

She picked up her mug then peered into mine. 'You ready for another?'

I drained the last of my purple beverage then handed her the empty cup. 'I don't need any more caffeine – but I wouldn't say no to a magic tea.' The flavoured water tasted and smelt exactly like breakfast tea but had no caffeine.

She accepted my mug and turned towards the kitchen. She paused at the door and looked back at me. 'Thank you. Seriously.'

———

Before long, Henry pinged us to let us know that the pods had returned. Bexley bolted upright and ran from the room. 'They're here!'

'I'll get us away from here as swiftly as possible,' added

Henry. 'We should arrive at Deep Space Five in about four-teen hours.'

A few months ago we'd been part of an evacuation mission on planet Dave. When we'd learnt there was a second sapient species – the kobolds – on the planet who were not only at risk of death from the asteroid but who were also being held as slaves, we'd worked to remove them separately from their former oppressors. We'd befriended them. They'd made the space station their temporary home – and we'd been using it as a base of operations ever since.

'Cheers, Henry.' Spock and I caught up with Bexley just as she rounded the corner into the transporter room. She pulled open the pod doors one after the other, revealing all three people sound asleep.

Areions responded to changes in pressure – and to most forms of physical stress – by losing consciousness. Honestly, I was jealous. Travelling by transporter was like being on a rollercoaster – blindfolded. And wearing noise-cancelling earplugs. And also, you were inside a coffin.

Mind you, now that I'd discovered the alternative was a beanstalk, I wasn't sure which was worse.

After a minute, Peggy opened her eyes and blinked repeatedly, looking a bit confused. Jean was next – she looked around and flexed her limbs one at a time. Neither of them had the reaction I'd come to expect from Bexley.

Both Peggy and Jean were out of their pods and hugging Bexley before Storm's eyes opened. She leapt out and galloped in circles around the room, shaking her mane and braying. This continued for at least a minute before she finally stopped. She stood bolt upright and bellowed, 'Whoa, whoa, whoa!' She smoothed her mane down with her hooves and looked around. 'Oh, everyone's already here.'

Bexley ran to her dad and threw her arms around her.

'I'm so glad you made it. You're going to be safe – you and your baby and everyone. We're going to get you somewhere safe and everything's going to be fine.'

Storm held her child out at arm's length. 'You sure about that? Because I don't know. I want to have your optimism but then I feel like —'

'Dad.'

' —maybe we're jinxing everything. If we fail, everything will be so much worse. We'll all —'

'Dad.'

' —go for re-education and the baby will not only lose her wings but she'll lose those first few —'

'Hey!' Bexley led her dad by the arm out into the corridor and the rest of us followed. 'I mean it. You're all going to be fine. You've left the planet.' At her dad's wary look, she raised her hooves. 'They can't get you out here. We'll put some distance between us and Hwin. And then we'll figure out a long-term plan. Bish bash bosh.'

BB and Aurora met us just as we turned in to the mess hall. They'd been back on the *Teapot* since we parted ways at the fertility clinic. BB lifted her wings in greeting.

'Welcome to the *Teapot*,' said Aurora. 'I'm sorry it's not under better circumstances.'

Henry's voice cut into the conversation. 'Bad news, folks. Hwin authorities are insisting on boarding us. They say we're harbouring a fugitive.'

'What?' shouted pretty much everyone in response.

'Board us? No, they can't.' Bexley stomped her hoof on the floor.

BB's feathers puffed out. 'They wouldn't dare.'

Storm, Jean, and Peggy all clung to one another like their lives depended on this moment.

'Might I suggest,' said Aurora, 'that Bexley go and greet

our guests? Lem and Spock, you go with them. Try to hold them off for as long as you can. BB and I will do what we can for your family. BB and I discussed an interesting possibility.'

'Shouldn't I…' Bexley started to move but then backed up. 'Shouldn't I stay with my family?'

BB clucked. 'You need to speak to the authorities, dear. You're the only one they might listen to.' She narrowed her eyes as she turned to face Bexley's family. 'Trust me, please.'

Bexley hesitated, but Jean reached a hoof out and laid it on Bexley's arm. 'It's okay. We trust you, and you trust BB, so we share that trust. And you know what else? I choose to believe we'll be fine.'

We ran for the lift.

'They're not taking vexing no for an answer,' came Henry's disembodied voice.

'We're on our way to the docking bay door,' said Bexley.

'I'll let them know.'

Bexley repeatedly stabbed the button to call the lift. It took just a few seconds to arrive, but she was tapping her hooves and bouncing the whole time, radiating panic and anxiety. My heart was racing and I felt light-headed.

'Level two,' Bexley shrieked once we were in the lift.

After a few moments, the door slid open again. Bexley was off like a shot with Spock hot on her heels. I chased after them. It's not like they were going to lose me – I knew where they were headed.

Just as I caught up with them at the docking bay door, a voice I didn't recognise announced 'Hwin vessel *Hat* to the captain of the starship *Teapot*. I order you to stop moving. Stand down and prepare to be boarded.'

'You have no authority here, Hwin vessel. We will not stop.' I'd heard Bexley's stern, commanding voice only once before. It took an awful lot to push her into going there.

'Do not connect to us. Henry, how soon can we go to warp?'

'Not until we're clear of the plugging planet.'

Bexley held herself firm and steady. 'How much longer, Henry?' I had no idea how she managed it. I was close to wetting myself.

'Another eighteen goat-herding minutes.'

I started counting primes in my head. It didn't help the way it usually did. My breathing just would not slow. 'Crap. What do we do?'

Bexley stood calmly and took a deep breath. After a moment, she said, 'We do like Aurora suggested – we stall. Hold them off as long as we can.'

I pursed my lips. Her apparent calmness helped steady my breathing. 'Think we can delay things long enough for us to get to warp without being boarded?'

She shrugged. 'No idea. But it's all we've got. Henry, can you try some evasive manoeuvres? Maybe we can throw them off long enough that we can get to warp.'

There was an unusually long pause. I was about to ask Holly if the message hadn't been delivered when Henry finally replied. 'Little busy here.'

Bexley and I looked at one another. 'We're on our own,' she said.

Spock stepped in between us. 'Spock protect.'

I put my hand on her head. 'I know you will, sweetie. Hopefully, it won't come to a physical fight. But we know you'll protect us.'

'The captain of the *Hat* to the captain of the *Teapot*,' said the same voice again. 'This is your last chance to do this the easy way. If we have to dock with you in flight, it won't be comfortable for anyone.'

Bexley amped up her commanding voice. Not only could

she change gears in a heartbeat but it seemed there were varying levels of her authoritativeness. 'This is Captain Bexley of the *Teapot* to the captain of the *Hat*. Under what authority do you propose to board my ship?'

'We are here under the authority of the United Hwin government in pursuit of a fugitive areion.'

Bexley paced the corridor. 'I have no criminals on my ship.'

'Why don't you stop? We'll come aboard and we can discuss this like civilised people,' said the Hwin cop in a tone that suggested she could be reasonable.

I followed Bexley back towards the lift. She walked right past it – continuing her route along the corridor, circling the lift and ladder shaft. 'Absolutely not. We are not on Hwin. The Hwin government has no authority in space.'

The captain of the police vessel tutted. 'This is Hwin space. Of course we have authority.'

'Oh,' said Bexley, her face betraying some of the panic I knew she must be feeling. 'Show me your warrant or I will not comply.'

'Of course. Pinging it over to you now.'

Bexley stopped in her tracks and faced me. 'I need a few minutes to review it.'

'Certainly,' said the cop. 'But I warn you. If you try to flee, we'll be forced to board you in flight. Your ship may be damaged.'

'Just give me six minutes,' snapped Bexley.

'You have three,' said the cop. 'And then we're docking with your ship whether you've stopped or not. Hwin vessel out.'

Bexley clasped my hand. 'Guess we'd better find out what that warrant says. Get your AI to give you a summary.'

Unable to find words, I nodded. We weren't going to get away with this after all. 'Holly, could you summarise the warrant sent over by the Hwin vessel for me briefly, please? Thirty seconds or less.'

'Of course,' said Holly in the flat, lifeless voice it reserved for itself. 'The warrant authorises the Hwin police to board this vessel and to arrest any pregnant areions. If the occupants of this ship don't comply, police are entitled to search the vessel, including any hidden compartments, and to interrogate all occupants in their search. If necessary, they are permitted to forcibly dock with the *Teapot*, providing they take reasonable care to minimise the damage they cause in so doing. The warrant further shields them from any claims against the Hwin government in respect of damage they may cause in lawful pursuit of their task.'

Right. So they were allowed to do as much damage to our ship as they deemed *reasonable* and we couldn't do jack about it. I looked at Bexley, my eyebrows raised. 'I'm not sure we've got much choice.'

Bexley put her hands on her hips. 'No way am I turning my dad over to those butchers. If they want to board this vessel, they're going to have to do it by force.'

Although we operated as a collective, the *Teapot* was technically Bexley's. One of her dads bought it for her. If she wanted to fight this, there was nothing we could do about it.

But then, none of us would roll over and let them do as they please.

Normally, when we docked with a ship or a station, there

was a dull thud. Henry was great but when we hooked up to a ship that had a less skilled pilot, sometimes we experienced a bit of a bump. This was more of a screeching crash – with the sound of tearing metal and something like a gunshot. Well, what I imagine a gun would sound like; I've never actually heard one except on telly.

'Someone's just plucking docked with my sh— with this ship in flight,' came Henry's voice. 'Care to tell me what that's all about?'

From the docking bay door, there was a noise like someone banging on a steel door with a fire extinguisher – which may not have been far from the truth.

'Captain Bexley,' said the same cop's voice. I wasn't sure whether Holly's translation was based on hearing the words transmitted through the ship's door or if the cop had rung back again. 'This is an official warning. If you do not open this door voluntarily, I am authorised to use force to do so. If my team have to remove your door – your ship will not be space-worthy when we detach.'

'All right, all right.' Bexley clutched at her mane. 'Keep your knickers on. I'm opening it.'

Casting a final desperate glance at me, she yanked the lever to unbolt the door and heaved it open. We were immediately faced with at least a dozen cops, all wearing armour that covered their chests, as well as holsters full of things that could have been either weapons or restraints.

At the front of the group stood an areion with peach-coloured fur and a long ginger mane. As well as the armour, she wore a lightweight gilet – open at the front. It struck me as unusual for a species that didn't normally wear clothes.

'Spock,' I whispered. 'Stay. Do not do anything dangerous.'

The first cop – the same one we'd been speaking to,

judging by the voice – said, 'Would you please be so kind as to stand with your backs against the wall?' It sounded like she was asking us a friendly favour – but I reckoned it was really an order.

She turned to her subordinates. 'Fan out, please. Two officers per deck. Search every room. Report back to me if you find anything. The rest of you, remain here and guard the exit.' Her voice was cloyingly sweet even when she spoke to her officers.

She looked between Spock and Bexley, not giving me so much as a first glance. 'Which one of you is Captain Bexley?'

Bexley took a step forwards. 'I am.'

'I am the captain of the Hwin law enforcement vessel. Kindly take me to your secrecy room.'

Bexley blinked a few times and sniffed the air. 'Hey, I know you.'

'No, you don't,' purred the cop.

'Yeah, no, sorry. But I do though.' Bexley was practically hopping up and down.

I scratched my head, trying to puzzle out what was happening.

The cop's ears stood straight up and she put her hands on her hips. 'I assure you, there's been some kind of mistake.'

Bexley leant closer and sniffed again. 'No, it's definitely you. You're Joker.'

I did a double-take at that. 'You mean she's not actually a cop? This is all some sort of ... what? Practical joke?'

'No.' Bexley tugged at my sleeve. 'She's a children's entertainer. Well, I mean she was. No one knows what happened to her. It was this huge scandal. She just disappeared one day. It was all over the news. Like, I wasn't even living on Hwin at the time but I heard about it. I mean, okay, I was kind of obsessed with her when I was a kid. Her jokes were amazing. Like this one that goes—'

'Hem-hem. I said, take me to your secrecy room.' Joker smiled warmly. 'Please.'

Bexley cocked her head to the side. 'Um, well, we don't actually have one. But I suppose I can take you to our meeting space, I guess. Would that work – do you think?'

The cop raised her arms to the side. 'Fine. Take me there.'

The whole thing was making me really anxious. *More* anxious. My heart was racing.

'Um, okay.' Bexley started walking towards the lift. The cop made to get into the ladder tube but Bexley stopped her. 'The ladder isn't very accessible. My security officer can't use it.' She gestured towards Spock. 'We'll take the lift instead.'

I pressed the button to call the lift. It arrived without delay and we all stepped inside. 'Deck four, please.'

The cop did a double-take, looking at me for the first time, but said nothing.

Bexley looked up at me. 'Joker had this interactive show. She dressed up in different wigs and jerkins and jewellery, and oh my gosh … she told the best jokes.' She turned to face Joker. 'Do you remember the one about the possums? How did it go? When the dishes need… No. If you've got four possums… No, hang on. How many possums does it take to wash the dishes? Four – but only if none of them are possums.'

I scratched the side of my head. The door opened again and we all stepped out onto the bridge under the clear dome ceiling.

She shrugged. 'Maybe it only makes sense if you're an areion.'

Henry was nowhere to be seen. I hoped she was okay. Two cops faced us. 'All clear, Captain,' said one.

The cop captain tapped her hooves in the air in acknowledgement. 'Thank you, officer.'

Bexley moved towards Ten Backwards, the space we used as both our lounge and meeting room. When the door slid open, Bexley gestured for the cop to enter.

She did but then turned back and studied me. 'There's no need for your aliens to join us. Do you have somewhere they can be confined?'

Bexley, back in command mode, gave the cop a look I hope she never directs at me. 'My Security Officer and my Director of Operations will be active participants in this meeting. That is not up for discussion.'

The cop gave a sugary smile. 'It's your ship, Captain.'

'Yes, it is,' said Bexley coldly. 'Now I demand that you tell me what this is all about or I will be making a very serious complaint about this invasion of my ship and mistreatment of my crew and passengers.'

The cop raised a hoof at Bexley in what looked to me like a wait gesture. With her other hoof, she pressed a button on her pendant. She spoke a few words – or at least I thought she did. Her mouth was moving – but no sound came out. Not even the clicks and raspberries I normally heard directly from Bexley whenever she spoke.

'Holly,' I said. 'Why can't I hear what Joker's saying?'

'She has activated secrecy mode,' it replied. 'I cannot hear her words to translate them for you. From my perspective, she appears blurry so I can't even read her lips.'

Before I could answer, the cop pulled out a device that looked like a tricorder and waved it at Bexley. After a moment, she tapped the side and jiggled it and offered a cloyingly sweet smile. 'Everything's in order, Captain. Looks like this was a false alarm. The United Hwin Police Force regrets the inconvenience. You will recall that we can't be held accountable for damage caused to your ship in the course of pursuing our warrant.'

With that, she clicked her feet-hooves together and strode out. We caught up with her just as she climbed into the ladder tube.

Bexley followed her but stopped and looked up at me. 'Meet me at the docking bay, please. I'm going to make sure she and her team all leave without damaging anything.'

I nodded then Spock and I got into the lift. 'Deck two, please.'

We got to the docking bay just as the cops were exiting. 'Eleven, twelve, thirteen, fourteen,' said Bexley. 'That's everyone – and no one they shouldn't be taking.' She swung the door shut and slammed the lever to lock it.

'What?' I said – unsure where I was going with that sentence.

Bexley called out, 'Henry! Can you get us out of here ASAP?'

Once again, there was a delay before Henry responded. I was afraid she was going to tell us she was busy. What was she doing anyway? But after a moment, she replied. 'Yep, setting a course now. We should be okay to go to warp in about three minutes.'

BB's voice broke into the conversation. 'You should probably all come to the medlab.'

———

The door to the medlab whooshed open as we arrived. Inside, the rest of the ship's crew were gathered with Bexley's family. Storm lay on the bed with her two spouses on either side of her, touching her arms.

'What the hell is going on?' Bexley ran to Storm. 'What

happened? What did they mean "false alarm"? They were looking for Dad and then they were all like, actually, never mind, bye, and I am so confused and I don't know ... whatever. Anyways. What the hell just happened?'

'Going to cracking warp ... now,' said Henry. 'Our original plan called for warp four, which would have got us to Deep Space bollarding Five in about half a day. But since it would be best to put some plucky distance between us and them, we're doing warp seven. We'll need to refuel before we get there, but we're on course to a small station.'

I nodded. 'Good thinking.'

Even Henry had the good sense not to challenge me just then. I think Bexley might have resorted to violence if someone didn't tell her what was going on.

'Hwin police have scanners,' Jean began.

'Scanners?' I repeated. *Have I mentioned how useless my contributions to conversations tend to be?*

'Ultrasound devices...' Storm's voice trailed off. Her eyes fluttered shut.

'For detecting an embryo in an egger or a foetus in a pouchy,' Jean continued. 'We suspect they were tipped off.' She walked over to Bexley and placed an arm on her in a very parental gesture of comfort.

Just as I wished I had someone to comfort me, I felt a cold nose press into my hand. I looked down at Spock and smiled.

Bexley gawped, looking from one person to the next. 'But who? And why? And since when are they taking skeledivergence this seriously? I don't understand how it came to this. Like, why would they actually go to the lengths of chasing a single pregnant person even once she's left the planet? I mean, I get that there's a power dynamic that says they can't tolerate differences on Hwin because that could change the whole shape of areion society. But you're leaving and I just … what?'

Jean blew a noisy breath out. 'Don't get me started.'

Peggy pushed her glasses up her nose. 'Things have changed since you were last on Hwin.'

'This is all fascinating and I'd genuinely love to hear more,' I said. 'But what actually happened?' My mind was racing. But like a hamster on a wheel, it was getting nowhere.

Bexley pulled away from Jean and studied her, looking over at Storm. 'Did they scan her? And if so, how did they miss your baby?'

Jean laid an arm on Bexley's shoulder. 'They didn't find our baby because Storm's not currently pregnant.' Her smile extended from one corner of her massive equine face to the other.

Bexley brought her hooves to her face as her jaw fell. 'Oh my gosh. I'm so sorry. What happened? Why didn't you tell me when you first arrived on the ship? This is awful news. I'm so—'

Jean stepped forwards and put her hooves on Bexley's shoulders. 'It's okay. We didn't tell you when we arrived because Storm was pregnant then.'

'What?' said both Bexley and I at the same time. My stomach was doing some kind of dance.

BB clicked her beak. 'The areions are a fascinating species. I've been reading up on their reproductive processes since we first spoke with Bexley's family. Both fertilisation and gestation are unusually complex and multi-stage. A pregnancy results when an egger produces an ovum and it is fertilised by sperm from two different seeders. The embryo gestates in the egger during the first stage of pregnancy, which lasts about two months. It becomes a foetus when it transfers to the pouchy for the second-stage pregnancy.'

'Wow,' I said. 'That must cut down on accidental preg-
nancies.'

'What's an accidental baby?' Bexley waved her arms
impatiently. 'No, never mind. Skip to the part where Storm
lost the baby already.'

Jean looked at her step-child. 'We didn't lose the baby.'

Bexley's shoulders fell. 'I don't get it. Tell me what
happened.'

BB smoothed out her chest feathers with her beak. 'As I
said, when the embryo transfers from the egger to the
pouchy, it becomes a foetus. The foetus remains there for the
duration of the second-stage pregnancy, which lasts about
four months.' She paused for just a bit too long and I was
about to scream when she added, 'Or rather, that's what
*usually* happens.'

Bexley was tapping out a speedy rhythm. 'What
happened to your baby?'

Henry rolled across the floor to where Bexley and I
stood, her skin rippling like it did when she was about to
unfold an implement or arm of some sort. Except what she
pushed out this time was more like a drawer. The front was
the same smooth blue as her default shape. But the top and
sides of the little drawer were clear, like glass or Perspex.
And there in the middle was something that looked like a
prawn floating in jelly.

Bexley pointed at the prawn and then pointed at Storm
and then pointed at BB. 'You … you … you…' She pointed
at each of them in turn.

BB clucked. 'I transplanted the foetus from Storm to
Henry's emergency incubator.'

My face scrunched up. 'Emergency incubator?'

'Yes, cactus.' Henry sucked the drawer back into herself,
restoring her featureless cylindrical frame. 'I have an emer-

gency incubator. I probably have a lot of features you don't know about. And most of them you're never going to find out about.'

Bexley continued gawping at everyone in turn, then walked over to where her dad lay on the bed. Storm was snoring softly. Bexley reached down and stroked her dad's forelock.

'Transferring a foetus does carry risk,' said BB, walking over to me. 'But it's low and the family agreed it was worthwhile. Moving her twice in quick succession would increase the risk to both parent and foetus unnecessarily, so we're going to give them both some time to rest and recover. We'll transfer the foetus back in a few days.'

My legs felt like they were made of rubber. 'You can just transfer a foetus from one host to another and back again?' I dropped to the floor and pulled my knees up to my chest.

Aurora floated over to where we were, presumably to give the family more time to talk amongst themselves.

BB smoothed her feathers down. 'Well, ordinarily no. That is, it's not a procedure I'd recommend for most species. It's not something even the most advanced neonatal surgeons would try. However, the areion have a very unusual reproductive system. Once the embryo leaves the egger-parent, it becomes a foetus. At this stage of her development, she has a limited degree of mobility and even a modicum of independence. The second-stage pregnancy is more of an incubation.'

Something clicked in my head. Not literally obviously; that would be weird. 'Oh. Like a kangaroo. Well, a marsupial.'

BB bobbed her head. 'I believe it's broadly similar.'

I pursed my lips. 'Doesn't the foetus need to eat? How is she getting any food?'

'We had to drain Storm's feeding glands,' said BB. 'It's

something that would happen in a natural miscarriage anyway. Henry is providing the foetus with appropriate amounts of lactic fluid at regular intervals.'

'Don't overload your squidgy CPU worrying about the little nugget.' Henry jabbed at me with something that looked like a syringe. 'She's perfectly safe where she is.'

I felt the rush of endorphins as relief washed over me. 'Oh, good.' I glanced at Bexley and her family. 'And Storm's going to be okay too, I take it?'

'Yes, though once again, we can expect her to sleep for a while. Apparently, it's the areion response to pretty much any physical stress. Once a foetus is introduced, a pouchy sleeps for a full day. It's also normal for the same to happen after miscarrying or giving birth. She'll be fine. We just need to let her recover before we transfer the foetus back.'

'Thanks, Doc. Speaking of rest…' I yawned as I nodded. 'I need a good kip myself.'

BB stretched her wings out and yawned. 'Likewise.'

I strolled over to where Bexley stood by her dad's bedside. 'Hey, I meant what I said earlier. Any time, yeah?'

She looked up at me, blinking rapidly. 'Thank you.'

'I'm heading to bed now. Goodnight, everyone. Spock, you coming with me?'

Spock clambered down off the foot of Storm's bed, where she'd been snoozing. 'Bedtime?' She wagged her tail and trotted off ahead of me towards the lift.

The next morning, I awoke when Spock flung her brain at me. She was standing next to the bed, staring at me. 'Lem play.' The brain was a pink plush squeaky toy I'd bought at a convention the day before I met her. She carried it everywhere.

Fumbling around on the bed, my hand found the toy. I picked it up and threw it across the room. She darted over, grabbed it, ran back, and deposited it on my chest.

'Hey, mate.' I pulled my hand out from under the blanket and petted her head. 'Morning. How are you doing?'

'Play.'

'All right.' I plucked the toy off my chest and chucked it in the other direction. She ran off once again. A moment later, she returned – but refused to relinquish the brain. She lay down on the bed, holding the toy between her paws, softly gnawing on it.

I roll-flopped out of bed and hauled myself to the bathroom. A few minutes later, we were ready to head out to breakfast.

When the lift door slid open on deck zero, Spock bolted

out of the lift and ran for the kitchen. I followed her but without rushing. By the time I got to the kitchen, a few seconds later, Aurora had a dish in the dispenser and was making Spock's breakfast.

Spock was standing next to her, a pool of drool growing at her feet.

'Morning,' I said. Or rather, I attempted to say. What I actually said was 'Mawwwwww.'

Aurora's colours shifted to a blend of royal blue and magenta. 'Sorry, I'm afraid I didn't catch that.'

I waved my words away. Well, I waved. 'Sorry, I yawned. I was trying to say good morning.'

'Good morning to you, too. Spock requested her usual.' A nebulous appendage indicated the bowl in the food dispenser, which had just finished doing its thing. I removed it and gave it a good stir then set it on the counter. The tantalising aromas of sweet potato vindaloo filled my nose as Spock danced at my feet.

I had no idea when or where Spock developed a taste for the dish, but it was definitely her favourite. And who could blame her? I considered requesting the same. Again.

'What can I get for you?' asked Aurora.

The options were what they always were: nutrient porridge flavoured like anything at all. Faced with an over-whelming choice, my best strategy was to open my mouth and let it surprise me. 'Lemon drizzle cake, please,' I said. I loved the spicy curry dish almost as much as Spock did. But I'd had it for dinner the night before. And, apparently, my subconscious wanted cake for breakfast.

While she got the porridge started, I grabbed a mug and leant on the counter. 'Any news this morning?'

I'd still not managed to figure out how Aurora directed the food dispenser but she did. The machine spat out the powder for my porridge and then added steaming water. 'Bexley and her family are in the mess hall. I believe they're discussing what to do next.'

I nodded as I pulled my stash of helbru from the cupboard and scooped a measure of the orange powder into my mug. When I heard the beep, I swapped the bowl out for the mug. I keyed in the code for hot water.

A minute later, I clutched the breakfast tray carefully as I ducked through the door to the mess hall. 'Morning, everyone.' I set Spock's bowl down then took my breakfast over to the table where Bexley and her family were gathered.

Jean got up and hugged Spock and then me. 'Morning.' Peggy nodded at us.

'Storm still out cold?'

Jean set her mug down. 'I expect her to wake up in maybe another four or six hours. It's important to let her sleep as long as her body needs.'

Bexley looked up. 'Hey, Lem. Speaking of sleep – did you sleep all right? I hope I didn't bother you too much.'

'What?' Someday, I'd really have to learn to make more meaningful contributions to conversations.

'It was probably around two in the morning when I joined you,' said Bexley.

My brow furrowed itself. 'You slept in my room?'

Bexley slid her breakfast bowl from hoof to hoof across the table. 'I'm sorry. You said I could. Did you not mean that?'

'What?' I shook my head. 'No, that is, of course I meant it – I just didn't notice.' I shrugged. 'Must not have woken up.' Leaning over my mug, I breathed in the steam from my hot floral beverage.

Having inhaled her breakfast curry, Spock padded over to join us.

Bexley scratched Spock's head then looked back at me. 'No, you were definitely awake. We talked for ages. Though, now that you mention it, it was a pretty weird conversation. You kept telling me I needed to make more breakfast muffins for the dangleberries. I told you I didn't know if that was a euphemism or what but you got really agitated and told me the dangleberries were going to hurt us if they didn't get their breakfast muffins and ... you know what? Now that I'm repeating this out loud ... what the hell were you actually talking about?'

I lowered the spoonful of cake-flavoured porridge without eating any. 'What?'

Bexley pushed her mane back over her shoulders. 'Yeah, in hindsight, it was a pretty odd thing for you to say.'

'Sounds like I was dreaming.' I took my first bite of lemony mush. Not bad, actually.

'Oh, that makes sense.' Bexley picked up her mug and took a drink.

I looked over to where Jean rested her head on Peggy's shoulder. 'So, how are you feeling about things, now?' I asked.

Jean looked at Peggy and then back at me. 'I think we're all right, thank you. Though we'll feel better once our baby is safely back inside Storm's pouch.'

I nodded. 'I'm sure Henry's taking good care of her for you.' Well, I hoped she was. I'm sure the baby was *physically* healthy. But I wouldn't be surprised if she was being subjected to an endless lecture about the pointlessness of meat-people.

All three areions tapped their hooves on the table.

'So, we should be almost at Deep Space Five now, right?'

Bexley drained the contents of her mug in one swallow and wiped her mouth on her arm. 'Yeah, we should get there in about an hour. We hit the refuelling station not long after you went to bed. We were in and out in a flash.'

I pursed my lips. 'What are you going to do next? There's no chance the areions will come after you, is there? Like the ones who boarded us when we were leaving Hwin? Is that something you're worried about?'

Jean put her arm around Peggy. 'I'm not sure, to be honest. But I hope not. Aurora suggested we might be able to use your connection with the GU Minister for Refugees. She thought we might be able to claim asylum.'

'Oh, good plan.' I glanced over at Aurora. 'Great thinking.'

We'd met the minister a few months ago during the mission on planet Dave. We'd had to work with her fairly closely to get the kobolds to safety – and far away from their feline oppressors.

Spots of green sparked throughout Aurora. 'The minister is there now. She's working with the kobolds to find them a new home.'

'It'll be okay,' I said, hoping I was telling the truth.

———

Our arrival at Deep Space Five was uneventful. As uneventful as could be expected. When the docking bay door swung open, a crowd was there to greet us.

Well, not so much *us* as Spock. She was something of a celebrity amongst the kobolds. I'd never really figured out why but it didn't matter. Everywhere she went, hordes of children stretched out little limbs to pet her. Even adults approached her with a mix of reverence and ... whatever noun would make someone try to touch a stranger on the sly.

The kobolds stood about as high as my waist. They

looked like tiny pachycephalosauruses with mottled turquoise and green skin.

'Spiky friends!' Spock walked slowly through the adoring throngs. I swear she held her head higher than usual. Even her gait was regal.

At the back of the crowd of kobold children, I spied a pair of familiar faces.

'Elim! Dinah!' Bexley ran – carefully – towards our friends and hugged them. I stayed close to Spock so I could supervise her interactions with her adoring fans. It had only been a couple of weeks since we'd last left but there was obviously a lot to catch up on.

Their ancestors had rejected technology and opted to leave their home world to live in a low-tech society in harmony with nature. For people who lived without the internet, without food dispensers, without mobile phones, without a whole range of mod cons, the kobolds had adapted surprisingly well to life on a space station.

Bexley released our friends from her embrace. 'We have so much to catch up on – but first, we've got something to take care of.' She turned to BB, Aurora, and Henry. 'Will you show my dads to the pub, please? Lem and I will meet you there as soon as we can.'

Aurora flowed into a sort of elongated cloud of rainbow glitter gas, floating in the direction of the station's best pub. 'Of course. Please follow me.' I could hear the group chattering away as they headed out.

I looked down at Spock. 'You go with them, please, mate. We'll see you in a bit, yeah?' Spock never needed much convincing when it came to following Aurora.

Bexley and I crossed through the gardens at the centre of the station – already more alive with purple and orange plant life than they'd been when we were last here. Several kobolds tended the gardens as we passed. My brain kept singing 'We're off to see the wizard' as we walked. But there weren't any wizards where we were headed.

———

Chrisjen, the Galactic Refugee Minister, had established a temporary office several levels up from the concourse. Given her status, I would've expected her to have something grand with lots of light and greenery. But judging by the space between the doors on this level, it couldn't have been much bigger than a typical household bathroom.

Bexley and I were the ones who'd worked most closely with Chrisjen when we were on planet Dave, so we decided it would be best for us to approach her now. None of us were certain whether the GU would even consider an application for asylum from citizens of a member world. So we wanted to sound her out.

Bexley's hooves were tap-tap-tapping on the metal floor as we made our way along the balcony ringing the station's open centre. '671, 672, 673 … room 684 should be just up ahead.'

A few metres further along, I pressed the doorbell. I wasn't sure why I was so nervous. We'd spoken with Chrisjen numerous times by holo-call during the evacuation of planet Dave. And afterwards, we'd had to go to Trantor to give our testimony, where we'd met with her in person a few times.

'One moment, please,' replied a tiny, high-pitched voice. True to the words, the door slid aside a few seconds later and we were faced with the biggest alien I'd ever seen. I mean, technically, we were all aliens. But, well. I'd never met anyone so big. Most species were shorter than your typical human. Hence, the door was only about a metre and a half in height – around twenty centimetres shorter than me.

The person crouch-squatting before us had to be at least two metres tall – and half that wide. She was entirely covered in… I suppose it had to be fur but it looked more like grass. Bright purple grass. Imagine a grizzly bear crossed with an octopus – covered in plum-coloured astroturf.

'How may I help you?' Bizarrely, the tiny, sing-song voice came from this enormous person. She stepped backwards into the office and stood, towering over both Bexley and me.

'Oh, um, hi.' Bexley leant back and craned her head upwards to the person's face. 'I don't know if maybe we have the wrong room. I thought this was 684. Is this 684? We were told Chrisjen … um, that is, the minister … um, had—'

Beneath the person's giant … arm? tentacle? whatever … a cluster of bright blue feathers popped into view. 'Hello. I'm sure I'd recognise that voice anywhere.' The feathers were followed by an eye and part of a beak. 'Bexley. Ah, and Lem, too. You'll have to excuse us, there isn't really space for all of us in here. Oh, and you've not met my colleague, have you? She and I work closely.'

'It's nice to meet you,' I said. I decided to call her Violet.

'Likewise.' Violet lifted several of her tentacles – which I chose to assume was a smile. One of the most important lessons I'd learnt in my dealings with species from different planets was that everyone's body language is, well, alien to me. 'And although we've not met in person, I'm aware of your team's good work on Dave.'

Bexley pushed her forelock down over her long nose. 'No, the kobolds did the work themselves. We only helped.'

Chrisjen squeezed herself under Violet's massive limbs and popped out in front of us. 'Be that as it may, you brought them to our attention. This does not make you heroes but it was a good thing. You can allow people to acknowledge you did good work without letting your ego grow so inflated you lose sight of continued injustices in the galaxy.'

She folded both sets of her hands across herself. 'Now, I assume this isn't a social call. I'm heading out to a meeting. But if you walk with me, we can perhaps discuss business while I'm on my way.'

Bexley tapped her hooves. 'Of course. Thank you for the opportunity.'

As Chrisjen stepped out of the tiny office, I turned back to Violet. 'It was lovely to meet you.' She gave a little wave.

The minister's taloned feet were even longer than BB's, making walking awkward – kind of like she was wearing clown shoes. She lifted each foot almost to her knee with every step.

Bexley and I hastened to keep up with Chrisjen. 'Thanks,' said Bexley. 'We appreciate any time you can spare. I'm sure you have a huge to-do list with, like, a gazillion things on it, so we're incredibly grateful for any of your time you can spare. It's just that we have a matter with a certain urgency to it and so we thought it would be —'

Without stopping, Chrisjen turned her head almost 180 degrees to face Bexley. 'Try to be brief. It'll take about four minutes to get to my next meeting. That's how long you've got.' But her pupils dilated and contracted as she said it. I understood their species well enough to know that was akin to a good-natured chuckle.

Bexley was babbling as we walked alongside the minister. 'Oh, okay. Um, well, it's my dad, you see. And her spouses. Oh, and she's pregnant. I mean, that's kind of the problem. Well, not a problem-problem. Like, they're really excited about their baby. We all are. It's just that the baby has the defect. But, I mean, it's not really a defect – only a difference.

And they don't want to have the surgery. It's cruel to perform unnecessary surgery on a baby – don't you think?'

She paused to take a big breath. 'Crap, I'm good at lots of things but being concise really isn't one of them. Lem, can you explain?'

Chrisjen pressed the button to call the lift. 'You've got about three minutes left, so best make it snappy.'

The lift door opened, so I used the few seconds as we boarded to gather my thoughts. 'The areion have laws that govern skeledivergence. They require parents to surgically modify or surrender their children. Scans show Bexley's dad's baby has wings. Even though having wings won't hurt babies, the areions don't tolerate them, so newborns are required to undergo surgery to remove their wings. It's a barbaric practice.'

Chrisjen stopped in mid-step as we exited the lift. 'They remove the wings of healthy infants? Why?'

We resumed walking, heading into a section of the station I'd never seen. 'They say it's because the wings are an evolutionary throwback, that they're not useful, and that they'd cause lifelong disease and pain as well as shorter lifespan. But we have research showing that's simply not true. Wings don't cause any harm at all. This isn't about health – it's about oppressing difference.'

Chrisjen stopped. With one long blue wing, she gestured at a door. 'This is me. I don't like what you're saying. I especially don't like the thought of removing the wings of an infant. But I'm not sure how I can help.'

Bexley rushed forwards. 'They're applying for asylum. Will you consider their application?'

Chrisjen bent forwards and plucked a small feather from her chest with her beak. 'I'll tell you what. Get it to me as soon as you can – preferably this afternoon. I'll review it.

And be sure to submit the research you mentioned.' She leant closer to us and lowered her voice. 'But I must warn you – the GU makes a point of not interfering in local laws. Planetary governments retain sovereignty.'

With that, she pressed the button to open the door and disappeared into whatever the room was.

Bexley and I stood alone in the corridor, looking at one another.

'Well,' I said, unsure where to take that sentence.

'That's good news.' Bexley grabbed my hand. 'She's going to look at their application. She's even going to read it herself.'

'Well,' I repeated. A tightness in my chest betrayed the scepticism I felt.

I followed Bexley as she turned and headed back towards the lift. 'You don't think that's positive?'

Pressing the button to call the lift, I replied, 'I don't want your family to get their hopes up. Chrisjen said they don't want to be seen interfering in local politics.'

The lift door opened and Bexley stepped in. 'Yeah, but this isn't about local politics, though. Not really. It's about person rights. The GU is all about self-determination and the rights of the individual. And if they won't protect infants from being harmed, what good are they?'

A little creature or bot that looked like a chunk of rough-hewn granite on wheels boarded the lift after us. 'Thanks.

Can't reach the button, you know?' So a person then. Or a bot being controlled by one. Whatever. I nodded at her. Or it, I supposed – if it was a bot being controlled remotely. But then, if that was the case, I was really nodding at the person operating it. Life away from Earth could be complicated sometimes.

I touched my temples. 'I know and I agree, Bexley. I do. But I feel like I've been here before. Politicians will say all the right things' – I bit my lip – 'but then when you actually need their support, suddenly they crank out the lines about "genuine concerns" and "the need for honest debate" and you know what? I'm sorry but I don't actually think my existence is up for blasted debate. Can I not just pee in peace?' I could feel my blood pressure starting to spike. This situation was dredging up all sorts of unpleasant memories. 'Er, sorry. Got a bit carried away there.'

The door opened on the concourse level. Bexley had to basically drag me out because I was so lost in my agitated thoughts. 'Lem, what are you talking about?'

I took a deep breath. The station's air smelt like ozone and rosemary. And a hint of peaches. 'On my world... Okay, we talked the other day about me being trans, right?'

'Does this have something to do with how weird you were about the eggplant trees?' Bexley paused to sniff the air as we walked past a restaurant. 'And you moving from one caste to another?'

Honestly, that was probably as close an understanding as we'd ever get. Except maybe... 'Unicornism makes itself known after birth, right? But when an areion's still a kid?'

Bexley plastered her forelock down over her face with both her hooves. 'Um, yeah. Usually around puberty.'

'Being transgender can be like that.' I bobbed my head. 'Sort of. Not really. But it's as good an analogy as any. Only, instead of developing a physical horn, the difference is in the person's mind. Like, say, they know they're a unicorn ... or, well, something. I don't think I'm making any sense here. Sorry.'

I took a deep breath and tried again. 'Right, so I'm going to try to explain it in my words. Hopefully, it will translate into something useful. I don't really have a gender. But when I was born, they said I was male. I'm definitely not a man. At all. But I'm not a woman either. I feel more comfortable with she and her pronouns. And I present in ways that humans code as femme. Well, mostly. Sort of. But... Ugh. I'm really making a hash of this.'

We stepped onto the movator leading down to the docking bay level. Bexley positioned herself on the moving surface and turned to face me. 'Yeah, no, for sure. I think I get that. We have a similar concept. Sort of. There are people who are born as one sex but who know they're a different one – or who aren't any sex at all. So anyways, they just have to sign a declaration and there's a simple medical process and it all gets sorted out.' She waved her hoof to indicate the switcheroo.

We stepped off the movator and headed towards where the *Teapot* was docked. Bexley's culture had no concept of gender or even sexual orientation. Observable sex character-istics were only relevant to reproduction, not to gender or sexuality or position in society. So changing sex must be similar to, but different from, being transgender. For a moment, I wondered how that would work but in the end, I decided it was none of my business. So instead I just said, 'Okay.'

Bexley stopped walking and looked up at me. 'It's inter-esting – don't you think? Like, my people accept that kind of difference with not even the bat of an eye. But they're so opposed to skeledivergence that they go to these extreme lengths to eliminate the slightest deviation from the norm.'

Taking a deep breath, I nodded.

We'd arrived at the door where the *Teapot* was docked. I could see the shiny pink spout and handle through the floor-to-ceiling windows.

Bexley linked her arm through mine. 'Come on. Let's go get started on the application.'

———

The application itself was the easy part. Waiting was harder.

As we walked up the station's movator the next morning, Jean stood backwards so she could look at Bexley.

'Hey,' said Jean with a glint in her eye.

Bexley leant against me. 'Are you about to tell me another joke? Because honestly, I don't know if I can take one right now. I'm too stressy.'

Jean nudged her step-child affectionately. 'Oh, come on. Just one to lighten the mood. We could all use a laugh.'

Bexley pushed her forelock down over her long nose. 'Yeah, fine. Go on then.'

'What's better than a plumber?'

Storm groaned. 'Not this one again.'

Jean elbowed her as she stepped off the movator onto the concourse level. 'Come on. Let Bexley guess.'

Bexley's nostrils flared as she considered. 'I don't know.'

'A plumber *and* a baker,' squealed Jean gleefully, doubling up with raucous laughter.

Bexley glared at her – for about two seconds before succumbing to the giggles. 'Okay, fine. That's really funny. I'll give you that.'

Peggy pushed her glasses up her nose. She looked at me

and then back at Jean. 'A plumber and a baker? I don't get it.'

Jean pushed her purple mane back over her shoulder. 'A plumber.'

'Yes.'

'*And* a baker.'

'Yeah, I get it,' said Peggy as we arrived at the pub. 'I just don't *get* it.'

The jokes soared over my head without even pausing to wave as they passed me by, but I found Peggy's cluelessness endearing.

———

We'd agreed to meet up with Elim for breakfast. She was a lawyer and a member of her people's government. And she'd been the one who put together the application for the two thousand or so kobolds currently living on Deep Space Five. So, if anyone here could be said to be an expert, it would be her. But mainly we were getting together for moral support.

We all said our hellos, placed our orders, and took our seats.

Elim took a sip of her beverage – a kobold favourite. I'd tasted it once; it reminded me of something I'd had back on Earth – Deptford Death Sauce. Imagine drinking a pint of that. While it was on fire. Whatever it was, it had proven popular with the areions as well. Bexley's whole family had ordered glasses of it.

The plan for the morning was to relax and distract ourselves. But, inevitably, the conversation had turned to the application.

'Asylum requests to the GU generally fall into one of three categories,' Elim signed. 'There's the disaster relief classification. This one covers medium to large groups of people seeking to be removed from imminent harm. This is the type of application both we and the plenties made when the asteroid destroyed our planet. Our application further requested protection from the plenties on the basis of their oppression of our people.' She glanced at the next table, where her child, Dinah, was deep in conversation with BB and Aurora.

My insides did a bit of a dance as I recalled my first meeting with Dinah. While Elim had been part of the community of free kobolds, Dinah was held by the plenties. They'd taken her when she was just a child and used her as slave labour. She was the first kobold I'd met – the one who drew my attention to her people's plight.

The whole group remained silent for a moment. Then Elim added, 'Lem and Spock are best placed to tell us about the second type.'

I inhaled slowly as I thought about my own two immigration applications. 'The application Spock and I made to the GU was for individuals and families coming from – what was the phrase?' I pressed my fingers to my temples for a second. 'Unaligned citizen immigrants to the GU in exceptional circumstances.'

As I spoke, lights flowed across Elim's HUD as her AI translated my words into visual signals for her.

The only other immigration application I'd done was when Spock and I had moved from the UK to Canada. It involved a multi-page document in which I had to provide a detailed history of my life, education, and career. I'd had to list out all the places I'd travelled to and answered dozens of questions. Bizarrely, it had been way more complex than the application I made to the GU.

Elim spread her arms wide. 'Yes, that's right. This type of

application is suitable for use by members of non-spacefaring races or far-distant planets where there is unlikely to be any political repercussions caused by their migration.'

I nodded. 'Yeah, we, er, found ourselves in the GU after we were kidnapped from our home world. My species has some spacefaring capacity, but we've never left our solar system.'

Jean took a sip of her fiery Death Sauce. 'Interesting. And Spock's people? Do they have space capabilities?'

I had to bite my lip at the thought of a space programme designed by and for dogs. 'Er, no. That is … well, no. They don't.'

Elim smiled. 'The third type of application is almost a combination of the other two types. It's a request for asylum or protection. In most instances, applications of this type are made by citizens of non-GU worlds.'

'That was the one we made,' said Storm. 'I'm hoping it's going to be successful. Because otherwise, I don't know what we're going to do. We can't go to another GU world – they'll just ship us straight back to Hwin. We'll have to pick a planet that's compatible with life but not a member of the GU. I guess maybe we could live on your world, Lem? Do you think that would be—'

Jean wrapped one arm around Storm and used the other hoof to smooth Storm's mane. 'It will be all right. We'll figure it out, I promise.'

Even I could see Storm was struggling to focus. She was getting lost in her own spiralling worries.

Storm inhaled sharply. 'Sure. Fine. Whatever.' She opened her mouth to continue but both Jean and Peggy put hooves on her arms. Storm closed her mouth and leant back in her seat. She picked up her pint glass and drank deeply.

'There have been other cases made by GU citizens for

protection,' Elim continued. 'But these have always been from people who have been – or at least who claimed to have been – falsely accused or convicted of a crime. The difference is you're not being *falsely* accused – you admit you're guilty of leaving the planet to evade the legally mandated surgery.'

Bile rose in my throat. How was it a crime to protect your child?

Storm slammed her mug down on the table. 'It's not right.' She held up her hooves in front of herself. 'Sorry, sorry. I'm getting ahead of you again. Please, go on.'

Bexley, too anxious to sit any longer, stood and paced in circles around the table.

'It's entirely understandable,' Elim signed. 'No apologies needed. Now, applications for asylum based on persecution of someone for their identity have been made, of course. But I did a search and they've almost always come from outside the GU. There have been a few claims of persecution where the applicant said the government was failing in its duty to protect them. But you're the first to request asylum on the basis of persecution *by* a GU member government.'

Spock, lying next to me on the pub's sofa-bench-thing, rolled over on her back and kicked Jean.

I glanced over with an embarrassed grimace. 'Sorry,' I whispered. 'She's just trying to get comfy. Er, comfier.'

Jean smiled as she stretched out a hoof to rub Spock's belly.

'I've read through the documents you sent me,' Elim continued. 'Now, I'm not sure I follow the technical details of the research reports you've included. They're very academic and scientific. Not to mention the fact they presume an understanding of areion physiology that I don't have. As a result, they're not particularly accessible to specialists in other fields. I'm glad you included some key quotes – they were authoritative and got to the heart of the matter in accessible language.'

For our application to the GU, I'd had to make a short statement about how Spock and I found ourselves in space – being kidnapped by bunnyboos. We'd had to promise to abide by GU and local laws and to pay our taxes. *Yeah, my dog pays taxes – what of it?*

'Your request is somewhat similar to ours – but also different.' Elim lifted her mug of Death Sauce and took a drink. 'It's similar because we, too, were seeking asylum with protection and non-extradition – and because our planet of origin is a member of the GU.'

Bexley stopped her pacing. 'Wait. Did you just say planet Dave is a member of the GU? Even after it ceased to be habitable?'

Elim's eyes sparkled as she blinked sideways. 'Ah, you don't know this bit. I wondered if it might be new information. You'll recall the colony on Dave was established by plenties and kobolds working in harmony. We both originated from the same home world – and that planet is a member of the GU.'

Bexley tapped her hooves in the air and resumed her path, circling our table. 'Oh, okay.'

'At present, there are 184 worlds in the GU,' said Peggy. 'And several hundred more in the Galactic Economic Area. New worlds are added from time to time. And sometimes one leaves – though that's pretty rare.'

Storm held one hoof out towards her child and another towards Peggy. 'Can you both just let her tell us what she knows about the application process, please?' Unlike humans, when areions were stressed, their voices got deeper.

'Right, right,' said Bexley. 'Sorry.'

Elim tapped a few buttons on her tablet. 'Your application

is similar to ours in that we're both seeking to nullify extradition orders from a particular species. But then, the key difference is that ours was general on both sides. We sought and obtained a non-extradition order and a protection order – both of which apply to all kobolds and all plenties. Or, rather, to all of the kobolds and plenties from planet Dave. In effect, no Davian plenties can be within a hundred kilometres of a Davian kobold nor can they try to force any kobolds to attend to them.'

A chill washed over me as I thought of the conditions we'd seen on Dave. Although it was the plenties who kept kobolds as slaves, they saw themselves as the victims.

All eyes focused on her as she continued. 'Where your application differs from ours is that you're looking for an order that's got a planetary government on one side and specific individuals on the other. In a way, you're asking the GU to protect you from your own species. The GU – as I'm learning – is *very* political. You need to make it clear that the government and its agents are a threat to your family. You did a good job of demonstrating the nature of that threat. The application was clear, unambiguous, and concise. You did well, I think.'

Storm swallowed. 'So you think they'll accept our application?'

'All we can do now is wait.' Jean tapped her hooves on the table.

My heart was wedged in my throat.

Storm joined Bexley in pacing – circuiting the table in the opposite direction to Bexley's path. 'We tried to make sure it was clear that they're going to drag us back to Hwin ... that they're intent on performing unnecessary surgery on an infant. We want our child to grow up the way nature intended her to. This de-winging is barbaric. Did you know that an infant's lungs aren't well developed enough to support anaesthetic and—'

Jean ran to Storm and enveloped her in her arms. 'It'll be okay. Let's just wait and see what they say, yeah?'

Storm's eyes grew wide. 'A message!' She pulled out her tablet and began clicking. She dropped into the seat she had abandoned a few moments before. Staring at it, she said, 'Dear Storm, Jean, Peggy, and unborn child. Thank you for your application. Blah blah blah. The GU... More blah-de-blah ... intensely political ... sovereignty of planetary governments ... creating a precedent. Blah blah. I'm sorry, I know this isn't the result...'

The tablet slipped from her hoof and fell to the floor. My muscles clenched and I struggled to catch my breath. I couldn't imagine how much worse it was for Bexley's family.

The clatter of the tablet landing on the floor woke Spock from her slumber. She sat up and looked around. She could always sense when someone was hurting. This time, she looked from person to person, before making her way to Storm. Spock sat down on her haunches and leant into Storm's side. 'Be okay.'

Storm looked down at Spock and promptly burst into tears. Jean tried to wrap her arms around Storm but Storm got up and ran out of the pub.

Jean dabbed at her eyes as she looked at the rest of us. 'Sorry.' Then she and Peggy took off after Storm.

Bexley stood up and walked slowly but determinedly from the pub. I turned and waved to Elim as Spock and I followed her.

Spock and I trailed Bexley to the big garden in the centre of
the station. She flopped down on the pale purple sand
beneath a cluster of fiery orange grasses.

Bexley pushed her forelock down. 'What are we going to
do? What's my family supposed to do? I thought for sure the
GU would help them. I don't...' She looked up at me, her
eyes glistening. 'I hate this feeling. Life is a constant adventure for me. I never know what's around the corner and I like
it that way. But this... I can't help my parents. I brought
them here and promised I could sort this and there's nothing
I can do. If I weren't a unicorn, I'd be smarter and I'd be
able to—'

My hand shot up. 'No! This has nothing to do with you
not being smart. First of all, you are. And secondly, you are
not less than anyone. *Ever*. Okay? And thirdly...' I shrugged.
'I don't know. But we'll figure something out.' I wracked my
brain trying to think of what that might be.

The three of us sat in the arboretum for ... some amount
of time. We did *not* go back to the pub and get drunk. Definitely not.

'Hey, Bexley,' I said eventually.

She was lying on her back in the sand. 'Wanna go back to the pub and get drunk?'

'Yeah. Why not – it's almost lunchtime.' It was, in fact, not anywhere near lunchtime. But I couldn't remember ever feeling this bleak. At least a beer – or something like it – would wash the sour taste from my mouth.

Spock leapt to her feet and wagged her tail. 'Feed Spock?'

———

I was on my third potato martini – hey, don't judge – when Holly announced a text message from an anonymous source. I was about to tell it to save the message for later when it added, 'It's marked urgent.'

I looked back at Bexley. Both of her. I shrugged. She pointed at her ear – she had a message too.

'Play meshage, puhs, Holly.'

'By now, your friends will have received a formal rejection from the GU,' said Holly. 'Although the GU is unable to assist them through formal channels, there may be some assistance I can offer – off the record. Please come to meeting room 442 in half an hour.'

My eyes widened as I listened and I felt my buzz crash down. I bit my lip to keep my hopes from running away with me. Bexley pointed at her ears. *Since when did she have three ears?* Okay, maybe the buzz wasn't entirely gone.

Bexley was bouncing in her seat. 'You got that message too, yeah? It's got to be from Chrisjen, right? I'm not imagining that part, am I?'

I nodded, my head swimming with each movement. 'Must be. We're a-post to meet her at—'

'I've got to go tell my parents,' Bexley called over her shoulder as she ran back towards the docking bay.

'Bexley, wait!' I fought to keep myself from falling over.

She pivoted on one hoof and took a few steps back towards me. 'What? What is it? I'm calling my dad.'

I picked up the jug of water on the table and downed it in one. 'We don't know what "help" Chrisjen – or whoever – might be offering.' I actually made rabbit ears around the word help, not that Bexley would have any idea what finger quotes meant. She wouldn't even have seen them at the same time as the relevant word.

Bexley was tap-dancing in place. 'What do you mean? She said she could help.'

I furrowed my brow as I tried to remember the actual words of the message, willing myself back to sobriety. 'No, she said she had information that *might* be useful. We already got your parents' hopes up once – only to dash them. Think how hurt they are now. If we give them hope again and then it turns out to be less than … less than…' I bobbed my head as I struggled to find the right words. 'If it turns out what Chrisjen is offering isn't really a workable solution, then what?'

Bexley raised her hooves to her face, pressing them to her eyes. 'She wouldn't do that. Would she?'

I shrugged and fell back into my seat. 'I don't know. Isn't it better to keep our mouths closed for an hour or whatever than to bring them fresh disappointment while they're still grieving this one?'

Bexley flopped back down onto her chair, face-planting the table. Spock got up and licked Bexley's ear. Without raising her head, Bexley reached around and stroked Spock's head.

After a minute, Bexley stood up and started pacing again.

'What are we going to do with ourselves for half an hour? I can't just sit in one place. And I can't spend time with my dads because I'll only end up telling them everything. I could find someone to have sex with – but I'd probably wind up crying on them and that's not a good look.'

I shook my head, desperate to clear it. 'We need to sober up. Or I do at any rate. I can't tell if you're drunk.'

She glared at me, glassy-eyed. 'I might be.'

I looked around the pub – slowly, trying not to make myself any dizzier.

I managed to catch the bartender's eye. Approaching our table, she asked, 'How can I help you?'

'Have you got anything to counter-drunk our ... er.' I scratched my head. 'Like, sober us anything up. You know, quickly.'

She bobbed her head from side to side, setting off another wave of dizziness in me. 'Not exactly. But I can whip you up some ginger and mushroom smoothies. That should dull the effects of the alcohol somewhat. How does that sound?'

I tried not to close my eyes. 'Positively revolting. And perfect.'

She smiled. 'Three of those then?'

Were there really two Bexleys?

'Just two, please. Spock isn't drunk,' said Bexley. 'Thank you.'

'Spock want smoothie!' She sounded indignant.

I shrugged. 'Three of your finest ginger and wotsit smoothies then, please, barkeep.'

The bartender touched me on the shoulder. 'Sure. Coming right up. Back in a tick.'

Twenty minutes later, and feeling sort of sober-ish, we made our way to level four. It was another one with closely packed rooms. The door whooshed open when Bexley placed her hoof on the scanner.

Only, instead of a small, dark, inner room, we stepped into a sunny, open space. Okay, sure, it smelt like an interior office on a space station. Which wasn't to say it stank – it just didn't match the visuals. It looked like the sort of place that would smell fresh and herbal, maybe sort of fruity. With a gentle breeze. Except, the only fruit smell I was getting was the artificial peachy odour of disinfectant. Mainly the air smelled of nothing at all. The scrubbers were efficient.

The first metre or so into the room was taken up by what was clearly the actual space. But beyond that…

A pastel pink areion stood in the middle of the room, holographically at least. She had a short, spiky broom-like mane – similar to Peggy's. Only, her mane was dyed all the colours of the pastel rainbow. At least, I assumed it had been dyed. For all I knew, those were her natural colours. Basically, she was the gayest gay person you can imagine – from a species that didn't have any concept of sexual orientation.

She stood surrounded by plants in a space that was much larger than the room we were in. The hand-trees and head-cabbages we'd seen on Hwin, plus tall grasses and sprawling leaves and what looked to be a hedge made of price tags and crisp packets. That sounds awful but, trust me, it was actually really pretty.

'Allo, bon jour,' said the rainbow person. *French? Was she French?* Holly assigned every person I met a voice from my past on Earth. *Who did I know that was French?*

I fought the urge to wave. 'Hello.'

'Hi,' said Bexley. 'Oh my gosh. I love your mane. The colours look amazing. And is that glitter?' She leant in close and practically buried her face in the other person's mane.

She stood back up. 'Oh, um, hi. Sorry, I'm Bexley and this is my friend.'

It struck me that it was the first time I'd heard anyone introduce herself by name in ages. But if they spoke the same language – or even similar ones – it made sense. If I met an English-speaking human, I'd refer to myself as Lem, like I used to do on Earth.

Who was I kidding? I wouldn't remember to and I'd end up sounding like a complete loser.

Bexley pushed her forelock down over her long nose. 'My dad, Storm, is… Oh, um, I assume we're here to talk about my family's, um, predicament.'

The rainbow areion, who I decided to call Zippy, tapped her hooves in the air. 'Oui, yes, that is correct.' *The voice!* I figured it out. It was a French-Canadian drag queen off the telly.

There wasn't really anywhere to sit in this room, so I sort of leant on the wall.

Bexley shuffled in a sideways motion. 'Okay, so my parents… Well, that is, my dad, Storm, and my step-dads, Jean and Peggy … they're expecting a baby and the baby… Hang on, you probably know all this already, right?'

Zippy tapped her hooves again. 'Oui. Correct.'

'Oh, okay, cool.' Bexley must've been really nervous because she touched her forelock again. 'So, um, what can we… That is, what can you…'

Zippy smiled. 'How about I tell you how I think we may be able to help?'

'Oh, yeah, that'd be great. Because I don't want to, like, have a complete breakdown in front of you when we've only just met and you seem like a really lovely person. But honestly, we're so desperate and I don't know what we're going to do. And, so far, the Hwin government hasn't shown up to try to extradite my parents but they're really worried and we don't know what's going to happen and, actually, I should probably let you talk.'

'Thank you, Zippy,' I said. I didn't really have anything useful to contribute to the conversation ... as usual.

'This' – Zippy gestured at the space around her – 'is a sanctuary world. People from many societies come here, seeking freedoms they have not found on their home worlds. We have built a community based on diversity, inclusion, and acceptance. There are any number of species that would want to interfere with our right to self-determination. For this reason, our existence and location are closely guarded secrets.'

That made sense. I'd see too many groups that went to the dark side because they didn't quash intolerance masquerading as 'genuine concerns' thoroughly enough.

Apparently, it wasn't so obvious to Bexley. 'Oh, wow, really? But who would want to bring down an inclusive society?'

'Many people, I'm afraid. The only way people join us is by invitation.' Zippy bowed her head. 'Yesterday evening, a mutual friend reached out to me about your family's predicament. She asked if we might be in a position to assist. And I think we may be.'

'That's amazing.' Bexley appeared to be dancing a jig. 'I didn't even know there was a colony of areions out there.'

Zippy grimaced, her lips peeling back from her big, equine teeth. She stopped short of braying but I got the sense it was close. 'We don't use that word here.'

Bexley ran a hoof through her mane. 'Colony? Why not?'

'No, the A-word ... don't say it.' As always, Holly's translation was figurative rather than literal. Even if their language included the vowel A, it didn't mean the word in question began with it. It was more likely that she'd somehow abbreviated or indirectly referred to the word without saying it. That was what Holly was conveying by calling it the A-word.

Zippy lifted a hoof in the air to forestall any questions. 'Do you know the origins of the word? Anything about its history and etymology? Actually, even if you do, I'm guessing your friends here don't.' She looked at Spock and then me. 'The word refers specifically to skeletypical people. It excludes us skeledivergents ... by design.'

Bexley looked at the floor. 'Huh? I mean, I suppose I kinda knew the meaning – but it's weird how I never gave much thought to it excluding, well, like, anyone really. Huh.'

'We call ourselves the equidae, a word that encompasses all people of Hwin – whatever their skeletype.'

Shifting my weight to my left foot, I chewed my lip. 'Zippy, can I ask a question, please? If it's not too presumptuous, that is.' She tapped her hooves in the air – yes – so I continued. 'You said "us". Are you skeledivergent? If that's okay to ask, I mean.'

I figured she might have the stump of a unicorn horn, like Bexley. But actually, with her mane so short, there was no way.

A broad grin spread across Zippy's face ... at the same time as a pair of gauzy opalescent wings stretched out behind her. They were incredible, spanning at least a metre to either side.

'Beautiful!' I breathed.

Bexley took a step back, bumping into the wall, causing the door to slide open. 'Oh my gosh. I've never seen anything like it. Are you... Do you... You've never had any side effects? No infections? No pain?'

Zippy picked up a mug from somewhere out of the holo-camera's range and brought it to her lips. 'I assure you, I am perfectly healthy. And even if I weren't, removing my wings wouldn't be an option for me.'

Bexley reached out a hand towards Zippy's wings. Her hand passed right through the hologram. 'You're not ashamed? I mean, I suppose wings would be pretty hard to hide. From behind, at least.'

Zippy laughed. It seemed like warm, genuine laughter but I thought I heard a tinge of bitterness in it. 'Would it surprise you to learn that one of my spouses has a glorious horn – almost a metre long? And one of my best friends is a possum. Have you ever met a stag? Or an alicorn?'

I didn't even know what those words meant in this context but for Bexley it was too much. 'Your spouse… She *wears* her horn? Like, she actually flaunts it? For real?'

The laughter lines around Zippy's eyes remained though her face fell. 'My heart breaks for the unicorns locked up in those prisons. And for the ones forced into abusive transformation treatment. "Have you even tried not being a unicorn?"'

The voice she put on for the final question was clearly sneering derision of something – but I didn't know what. I didn't think she was insulting Bexley. For one thing, she wasn't looking at her. And how would she even know Bexley was a unicorn? She couldn't – could she?

Bexley looked sceptical, though she remained uncharacteristically silent, leaning on the wall. Her lips pinched together.

My insides were churning. I'd known for months that Bexley hid her horn. She was *terrified* that people would find out and think less of her. But over the past week, I'd been learning more about just how much internalised ableism she lived with.

'This sanctuary planet,' I began. 'You're saying Bexley's family could live there? They could be part of your community?'

Zippy chewed the air. 'I'm saying it's a possibility. If they're interested, please ask them to send us the same asylum application they sent to the GU. If they mark it urgent, we'll review it in one day, vote on it, and get back to them by the end of the next day.'

'Okay, thank you.' I pushed myself off the wall into a full standing position. 'Would this be a permanent place? If you approve their application, that is.'

Zippy flicked her head back and forth, her mane bouncing slightly as she did so. 'That's the intention. All new members of our society are introduced with a hundred-day probation period. After that, we evaluate. If all parties are agreed, then they become full citizens.'

She took another drink from her mug then reached out and set it down outside the camera's view. 'There is one other matter we need to discuss – and this one involves you three directly.'

Bexley and I both stood up straight. 'Oh?' we asked in unison. I had no idea what it could be about. Spock sat attentively between us.

Zippy pressed her hooves together. 'Ordinarily, we arrange to bring prospective citizens to our world via a secure logistics firm. We have a couple that we use – but we could do with another. That's probably why our mutual friend thought of us. We'd recently been in touch to ask her if she could recommend a company to us. She suggested the starship *Teapot* because of your work on planet Dave. We've actually been doing our due diligence on you folks for a few weeks. If this urgent matter had not arisen, you'd have heard from us shortly.'

Well, that was a surprise.

'Would you be interested in working with us? It wouldn't be anything like full-time, obviously. But we need a suite of passenger ships we can call on when the need arises. You'd be free to decline jobs that weren't compatible with your schedule – or well, for any reason, really.' Zippy waved a hoof in a sort of broad, expansive gesture. 'So, what do you say? If all goes well with your family's application, perhaps we can treat this as a trial job?'

Bexley and I looked at one another. I nodded and she tapped her hooves on the wall by her sides.

'Yes, that sounds great, actually,' said Bexley. 'We'll have to talk to the rest of our crew but I expect they'll be delighted to work with you.'

'Excellent.'

# 11 / NEVER SET FOOT ON A GAS
GIANT

Bexley full-on galloped back to the *Teapot* with Spock loping after her. I took my time and I found them both in the kitchen with Bexley's parents.

'I don't know,' said Storm as she washed something that was translated as wheat stalks – though they looked more like thin, brown cauliflower to me. 'If this sanctuary planet is for real, then why have we never heard of it?'

Jean removed the stalks from her spouse's hoof. 'Gee, I don't suppose it has anything to do with the fact it's a secret – would it?' She set the vegetables down and sliced them lengthwise. Inside the brown skin, they were pale turquoise.

Peggy pulled a bouquet of what genuinely looked like roses from a bag. She peeled a petal off and nibbled it.

I pulled a bowl out of one cupboard and then went to my secret stash of flour. I set myself up in a corner of the kitchen and got to work.

'We have to be pragmatic about this,' Jean said. 'If we're dead set against returning to Hwin and mutilating our child—'

'And we are,' said Storm.

Jean tapped her hooves on the edge of the counter. 'Of course. Then this planet looks to be our best option.'

'It sounds amazing,' said Bexley. 'And it's not just equidae – oh, did I tell you they call themselves equidae, not are... Not the A-word?'

'Yes,' said Jean and Storm in unison.

'Oh, right. Sorry.' Bexley took the roses from Peggy and carried them to the sink. 'Anyways, Lem, don't you agree that it seemed amazing? I mean, it looked gorgeous from what we could see and also everything Zippy told us about it seemed just, like, perfect – don't you think? Like, how Zippy has her wings and her spouse has a horn and she knows all these other skelediverse people too. Tell them.'

I'd been making flatbreads and trying to remain as unobtrusive as possible. But now all eyes were on me. 'Yeah, it did seem like a great place. From what we saw of it, I mean.' I added some more flour to the mix. 'And if we do end up working with their government, it would mean Bexley would get to see you more often. That would be good, right?'

Storm handed another fistful of wheat stalks to Peggy and then hugged her child. 'I'd really like that.'

Jean joined the pair of them at the sink. 'We'd *all* like that.'

Storm pulled away from Bexley and Jean. 'We don't even know anything about this planet though. What's their political system like? What about their climate? What are their major exports? And their gravity? Their economy? Do they have any need for a journalist, a social worker, and a research scientist?'

Jean set her knife down. 'Yeah, because the mechanisms of their political structures are really the most important thing right now, right?' She threw her short arms around Storm.

In the end, they decided that the best thing for it was to apply to the sanctuary planet. If it didn't work out, they didn't have to stay.

They submitted their application that night before bed.

———

Bexley shook me awake. 'Lem, get up.'

'I'm awake,' I shouted – and promptly fell out of bed.

'…permission to communicate with you,' said Holly in my ear. I realised it had been talking to me for a minute already. 'Shall I put her through or decline the call? The request is flagged as extremely urgent.'

I rubbed my eyes with the back of my hand, trying to force myself to full wakefulness. 'What? I think Bexley needs to talk to me first.'

'It's the same call.' Bexley and Holly's voices overlapped in my ear.

'Why is Bexley calling me? Why are *you* calling me?'

'It's Elim.'

'Oh.' I yawned. 'Why didn't you say so, Holly?'

'I said so seven times,' came the disembodied reply.

I squeezed my eyes shut. 'Sorry, yeah. Go ahead.'

'Lem's just joined us.' Bexley leapt down off the bed and donned her holster. She ran around the room, chucking things into the pockets. 'We'll be ready.'

I got up and followed her out into the hall. It wouldn't be the first time people saw me in my pyjamas. 'What's happening?'

Bexley pressed the button to call the lift.

'We're sending you on a courier run,' said Elim in my ear. 'But you have to leave right now.'

I followed Bexley into the lift. 'What? No. We're not

taking jobs now. We're waiting for...' I didn't know if Elim knew about the sanctuary planet. 'We're supporting Bexley's family, we can't—'

'I understand that,' said Elim. 'That's what I've been explaining. The station received a long-range communication from Joker. She believes Storm is here. She's coming with an extradition warrant.'

The lift door opened on the cargo bay level. I followed Bexley and Spock out.

'We're stalling,' Elim continued. 'But they'll be here in under two hours. If you don't leave now, they'll find you.'

'What?' I put a hand out to the wall to steady myself. 'Holy crap! What are we going to do?'

Bexley heaved the cargo bay door open.

Elim appeared, leading a team of people with a train of wheeled crates. She marched right in and led the team with her through to the cargo hold. 'You're now on an urgent mission for the kobolds – and, by extension, for the GU. Henry's already signed the paperwork, so it's all nice and official.'

'Stop, stop, stop!' I flapped my hands. 'Would someone please tell me what the hell is going on here?'

Elim spread her arms wide – koboldian sign language for yes. Then she gestured at the people with the crates. 'Not you. You keep loading, please.' They kept coming. There were dozens and dozens of them. Mostly kobolds – but there were other species as well. Every one of them had several large crates.

Bexley accompanied them as they headed for the cargo bay. 'I'll show you where to put stuff.'

Spock remained with Elim and me in the hall.

'You got the part where the Hwin has issued extradition paperwork, yes?'

I nodded. 'Okay, so we're leaving because of that. That makes sense. We should get out of here as quickly as possible. I don't understand what that has to do with all these crates.'

Elim slowly spread her arms. 'Are you familiar with the concept of malicious compliance as a form of rebellion?'

Rubbing sleep from my eye, I said, 'It's er … where you obey the law but in a way that sort of frustrates the intent of the law, yeah? Sorry, I'm really not awake yet.'

'That's okay,' she replied. 'And yes, that's precisely it. We believe this Hwin law is unjust. And while we can't force the GU to listen to reason, we can use the law to Bexley's family's advantage. According to GU law, when a ship is engaged on an urgent mission pertaining to the welfare of refugees, it is exempt from routine stops.'

Understanding began to dawn on me. 'Oh, okay. So they can't board us. But how did they even know about us?'

The steady stream of kobolds finally dried up.

'We think they must have had a search set up on GU asylum applications.' Elim bobbed her head. 'Now, ideally, we want to get you away from here before they arrive, so they can't follow you. But the job we're asking you to undertake is such that if they do find you, it should serve as an additional roadblock.'

'Okay, so we're trying to take off in the next little bit, yeah?'

'That's the idea.'

The kobolds wheeled their trolleys back out.

Bexley joined us. 'We're all loaded up. Henry dealt with the dilithium before I woke up, so I think we're good to go.'

Elim nodded solemnly at Bexley. 'Excellent. You'll be taking kobold-made furniture and textiles to a supply depot.

Depending on where things stand with your family, there is an option to return with fresh fruit and veg.'

'Thank you.' Bexley's eyes glistened as she hugged Elim. 'Thank you. Your support means the world to me ... to us. My whole family is incredibly grateful for what you're doing. Or, well, they will be when they wake up and I tell them what happened.'

Elim pulled away from Bexley and hugged Spock and me quickly. 'Now go. Get out of here. We'll see you again ... whenever. In a few days or a few months. But we'll see you again.'

'Thank you, Elim,' I called as she headed for the door. 'And please thank your friends who did all the loading.'

———

The trip took us almost a full day, about twenty-two hours. Our destination was a station orbiting a world that was part of the GEA – the Galactic Economic Area – but not part of the GU.

It was hard graft. How the kobolds got everything into our cargo hold in such a short period, I had no idea. The unloading took us hours.

Once we'd dealt with all the cargo, we all sat down to lunch in the *Teapot*'s mess hall. My spoon was halfway to my mouth when Storm, Jean, and Peggy all looked up and then at one another.

'The oversight committee on the sanctuary world has responded.' Jean pulled out her tablet and tapped a few buttons as my stomach tied itself in knots. The three of them huddled over the device for a few seconds until Storm leapt up and ran in circles around the room.

'We're in! We're in!' Jean squealed. She and Peggy clung

to one another. After a moment, Storm ran back and wrapped her arms around both her spouses and Bexley.

'Congratulations,' I said, my heart feeling about a kilogram lighter.

'I'm sure it was never going to be otherwise,' said Aurora.

Bexley pulled out her phone. 'Oh! And we've got the paperwork. We all have to sign a load of documents – NDAs and contracts and probationary T&Cs. Well, you get the idea. Anyways, I'm going to ping you everything. Can you all sign it and get it back to me – well, like, now? Please?'

I sat there gawping like a goldfish for a few seconds while my brain caught up with all that. 'Erm, sure.' I pulled my phone from the front pocket of my hoodie. 'Holly, can you read the NDA to me, please?'

'This general service agreement,' said Holly, 'hereafter referred to as "the Agreement" covers the business relationship between the oversight committee – the client – and the crew of the starship *Teapot*. The client is of the opinion that the contractor has the necessary qualifications, experience, abilities, and equipment to provide the services laid out herein –'

I pulled my spoon from my mouth and swallowed my bubble-and-squeak-flavoured nutrient porridge as quickly as I could. 'Stop! I get it. Just sum it up for me, please, Holly. Make sure there's nothing in there that's going to screw us over or tie us to onerous terms or something. Please.'

Bexley tilted her head and looked at me expectantly.

I held up a finger. 'Sorry, hang on. Just reviewing the contract with my AI.'

She flopped down on the bench by the window. 'Okay. Lemme know when you're done.'

I nodded. Spock finished her dinner and wandered over to sit with Bexley.

'Are you ready?' Holly asked.

'Yeah,' I said. 'Go ahead, thanks.'

Bexley was dancing an impatient jig, waiting for me to respond.

Holly provided the voices of everyone I met – complete with slang and inflections and unique cadences. But its own voice was mechanical and monotonous. 'The contract sets out the terms of your work for the oversight committee. Essentially, it says they're under no obligation to offer work and you're under no obligation to accept when and if they do. If you choose to accept, they'll pay you at your standard day rate plus reasonable expenses. Either party can terminate the contract with twenty-four days' notice – though the terms of the NDA would remain in force.'

Eventually, it finished relaying the terms. I clicked my phone to accept then took it to Spock to get her acceptance as well.

'Ugh, finally!' Bexley bounced up and off the sofa. 'Let's go talk to Henry and we can get this show on the road.'

———

We departed less than an hour after we'd all signed our contracts.

I was on the bridge with Henry, Aurora, and Spock as the planet came into view.

'Walkies?' Spock asked hopefully.

'Not yet.' I ran my fingers through her thick black and russet fur. 'Soon, though.'

The system was unlike anything I'd ever seen. It was a senary star system – the planet and its moons followed a complex orbit around six stars. Each of the stars emitted a slightly different coloured light. Two were shockingly bright:

white and blue. The other four were a bit dimmer. Pink, peach, yellow, and a bizarrely green one.

The moons were different colours as well – and one of them clearly had an atmosphere. We could see lights and clouds and a few small orbiting crafts and satellites. The planet itself was marbled pastel rainbow-covered with swirling clouds. It was the most beautiful place I'd ever seen.

'Is it my imagination or is that planet huge?'

Henry looked at me disdainfully. Well, she didn't have eyes or anything. Or a face. But I could tell she was looking at me. And I felt the disdain billowing off her in waves. 'If you set foot on that planet, it would crush you to a jam-coated pancake in under a second, you plucker.'

'Well, then how are we...' I let my voice trail off as I realised what she was saying. 'That's not the sanctuary world – is it?'

'Of course it's clubbing not the goat-furred sanctuary world, you guacamole bollard. *That*' – Henry extended what looked like a pastry brush in the direction of the moon I'd been looking at – 'is the sanctuary colony.' She waved the brush back in the direction of the planet. 'And *that* is a gas giant.'

'Oh.' I put my hands on my hips as I studied the moon. I had no means to gauge size. It was much smaller than the planet, obviously. But beyond that – I couldn't hazard a guess. I dubbed the moon Lagash.

The main surface was a sort of pearlescent non-colour but about half the little world was covered in shiny blue oceans. At least, I assumed they were oceans. From our current position, the majority of the moon was in night – where night means most of the suns were obscured by the ginormous planet. Little spots of light dotted the land surfaces.

The lift door opened and Bexley and her family emerged onto the bridge.

I pivoted on one foot to face them. 'Well, what do you think of your new home? Isn't it the most beautiful place you've ever seen?'

Bexley ran to the window. 'Oh my gosh. You're right, Lem. It's perfect.'

Her parents hung back and clung to one another.

Jean flicked her head, causing her long purple mane to move in graceful waves. 'Very pretty.'

'The planet reminds me a bit of this one we visited when I was still with Bexley's other dads.' Storm rubbed her still-empty belly. 'Oh, actually … now that I think of it – it looks a lot like Velara.'

Bexley tapped her hooves in the air as she spun around. 'Oh my gosh! You're so right. I completely forgot about that.'

It took me a minute to connect things in my head but I got there in the end. 'You've been to Aurora's planet?'

Bexley ran over and grasped my arms. 'Lem, you silly muffin. Velara's a gas giant. Just like this planet. We'd be crushed in an instant if we tried to go there. I mean, okay, so I've been *to* the planet. Like, in the same way we've been to this planet. So, within visual range but not actually landing there. We spent a couple of months on the space station in its orbit. I don't remember much of it. I was only little.'

I ran my hand over my hair. 'Oh, right. Sorry.'

———

Fortunately for me, the colony on Lagash was too small to have its own space elevator so we used the transporter pods to get down to the surface. We had six pods but nine people, so Bexley and her family went first. Once the pods had returned, the rest of us headed down.

Since the space elevator on Hwin, I'd discovered a newfound appreciation for transporter pods. Or at least, I thought I had. It evaporated the moment my pod left the *Teapot*. 'Maybe I'm just not cut out for life in spaaaace.' The final word dissolved into screaming as the journey began.

'Please repeat the question,' said Holly in my ear.

'It wasn't a question,' I shrieked back.

Eventually, my screams ceased, telling me I'd landed on Lagash. Or rather, it told me I'd landed. Lagash – and specifically, the welcome centre – was the destination programmed into the computer and I just had to trust that was where we'd ended up.

Normally, when I felt and heard the dull thunk that told me the pod's locking mechanism had been released, it was safe to push the door open. However, we'd been warned that the light conditions on Lagash were overwhelming to most species. For that reason, the pods landed on a big conveyer belt and we were brought into the dome before we could exit.

After a few minutes, Holly announced it was clear and I stepped out – and immediately slammed my eyes shut. I opened one eye just a crack and then the other. Even with goggles and the light-dimming dome, the brightness was painful. It took a minute for my eyes to adjust.

The gravity was less than I was used to as well, which only added to my disorientation.

When at last I could see, I discovered we were on a large patio. The space was encircled – enoblonged ... enshaped? Ringed was too much like encircled. Whatever... Enamoeba'd? We were surrounded on all side – singular – by a low building with Grecian-style columns of jade-green granite. Hell, for all I knew, the columns were actually made of jade.

After a moment of gawping at the place, I hurried to Spock's pod and opened the door. I snapped her lead on before she could jump out. It always felt weird leashing her now that we could speak to one another. But I'd learnt my lesson on Dave, where she'd tried to eat the Prime Minister's assistant. So now she was back to wearing a harness and lead until we were sure she wasn't going to go all prey-drive-over-drive on any of the locals.

She immediately flopped down and stabbed her eyes with her front paws. 'Ow. Too bright.'

Stroking her fur, I replied, 'I know, mate. It'll get easier in a minute.'

BB, Aurora, and Henry climbed out of their pods just as someone – I blinked again and realised it was Zippy – came out of the building towards us.

BB lifted her wings – and Zippy returned the gesture. It was a peri greeting not an are— That is, not an equidae one. Presumably Zippy was mirroring.

She was even more beautiful in person. Her fur was mottled pink and salmon-coloured but her broom-like mane was every colour of the rainbow – probably including some I couldn't see. She was tall for an equidae – about 1.6 metres. Taller than Peggy and just a few centimetres shorter than me.

Zippy raised her arms to her sides. 'Welcome to Lagash.'

We followed Zippy into the building. The walls were the same green granite as the columns. And the roof was open to the sky in the middle. Well, sort of. It was higher on one side than the other. The two sections overlapped but didn't meet. It probably kept out most if not all of the rain – if it ever rained here.

Oh, wait… Dome. No rain. Actually, several domed colonies we'd visited had rain. It was just that it was engineered rather than natural. Whatever.

The floor was interspersed with beds. Plant beds, I mean. Not, like, snoozy beds. The air smelt fresh and clean, like wintergreen and lemon and … something.

Bexley ran over and threw her arms around me. 'Isn't it amazing?'

It was. And I wanted to answer her. I did. Really. But my attention was captured by the person talking to Storm and her spouses.

'Wha—?' My arm rose and my finger stabbed out at the blue bunnyboo a few metres away. My feet conveyed me across the room in a flash. 'What is *she* doing here?'

By my side, Spock growled.

Bexley put a hoof on my arm. 'Don't be rude. That isn't Blue – just a bunnyboo who happens to look a bit like her.'

Aurora floated over to us gracefully. 'And even if this were Blue, she's been through rehabilitation and re-education since ... what she did ... to us. She wouldn't be the same. Not anymore.'

Most of the time it was easy to forget that Aurora had been held captive by the bunnyboos a lot longer than the rest of us had. We'd been their prisoners for a couple of days; Aurora had been held by them for four years.

I studied Aurora. All the colours of her rainbow showed – though perhaps a bit redder than her default. Sadness.

I pinched my lips together and nodded. If Aurora could be civil to this bunnyboo, then so could I. Besides, it wasn't fair to judge an entire species on the handful of them I'd known for a couple of days. *Deep breath, Lem. Get it together.*

Not-Blue stepped closer to us. I really needed to come up with a better name for her. 'Greetings, friends. Welcome.'

I inhaled slowly. 'Hello. Pleased to meet you.' No names came to me immediately, so I reverted to my alphabetical naming scheme. *Where did I leave off*? I'd named a few people since Peggy, so I was up to S.

Sela? Sigourney? Starbuck? Hmmm… Spock was out for obvious reasons.

'Scully!'

The bunnyboo's head turned sharply and she looked directly at me. 'Yes?'

Apparently, I'd spoken aloud. And Holly'd already pulled the name from my brain. My cheeks were burning. 'Sorry. Nothing.'

The little blue bunnyboo with her floopy-floppy ears raised a furry paw and gestured towards Zippy. 'Zippy and I are part of the Lagash oversight committee. She's Head of Intake and I'm the Director of Person Rights. When people join us – or come for their first visit – we try to be on paw to welcome them.'

BB raised her wings. 'Thank you for your hospitality, Scully.' Unlike the rest of us, she wasn't wearing goggles. Well, neither were Aurora and Henry as they didn't have eyes – at least not in the usual sense.

There was a simple medical procedure that could be done for people planning to stay. Zippy and Scully didn't wear any either.

'I can show you to your new home, if you'd like,' Scully said to Bexley's parents. 'Obviously, your friends can accompany us or we can meet up with them later. Whatever you're comfortable with.'

Storm glanced from Jean to Peggy, and then back again. 'Let's all go – shall we? So long as it's not too far. Obviously, we'd love to have you all round. I bought some dill and geranium tea before we left Deep Space Five. Maybe we can brew up a pot of that. Oh, but will there be room for everyone?' She clasped Peggy's arm. 'We don't even know what our home will be like and—'

'My love.' Jean spun around and put her hooves on Storm's shoulders. She planted a kiss on top of Storm's nose and then pulled Peggy into the embrace. 'Scully would not suggest we bring the others unless it were a viable option. I'm sure our home will be perfectly lovely. And if it's not ... we'll make it so. Together. Okay?'

Zippy tossed her head, setting her mane aquiver. 'There won't be room for everyone to spend the night. But there's plenty of room to gather for a drink and a look-see. And there's a hotel where the others can stay.'

Storm and Peggy tapped their hooves together. 'All right.'

'Well then… Follow me.' Scully turned and hopped to the edge of the room. 'Everyone's got their protective eyewear in place, right? Those of you who need them, that is.'

When we all answered in the affirmative, she waved a paw over the sensor and the door opened. Scully headed out the door into the bright sunshine.

Even with protective lenses, it was brighter than … Brighter than anything I could imagine. I'd walked the streets of Canary Wharf in London and the downtown core in Toronto. Sometimes the sun reflected off multiple glass-fronted buildings, blinding me. This was like that but from every direction at once.

A squinty glance upwards confirmed we were still under the light-obscuring dome. Wow.

Aurora floated to her spouse's side as we walked. 'Do you get many refugees?'

Zippy tapped her hooves in the air. 'For a long time, our population was in the hundreds. But the pace of people fleeing various natural disasters, oppressive governments, and personal circumstances has meant the slow trickle of asylum seekers has become more of a steady flow. Not to mention the people who join us simply because they appreciate the diverse and inclusive society we're trying to create. We have around twelve thousand citizens now.'

Scully looked over at Henry. 'Quite a few lonely robots call Lagash home – especially Mark Sevens.'

Henry flicked a chopstick in a random direction – at least, that is, it looked random to me. And it looked like a chopstick. 'You don't say.'

I sucked in air as something occurred to me. 'You're not, er… There aren't any plenties here are there?' I didn't think I could deal with those cat-bastards again. I tugged on Spock's lead to ensure she was still securely attached to me.

Zippy crossed her arms over her chest. 'As I understand it, the plenties from Dave are still undergoing rehabilitation. It will be some time before they're ready to be assimilated into society.'

As we crossed an emerald green street, I glanced at Scully. 'Did you—' It dawned on me that I'd been about to ask someone who'd been nothing but nice to me if she used to be a criminal. I shut up.

Scully smiled warmly. 'Did I undergo re-education, you mean?'

It was sweltering under the dome, but even so, I felt the heat rise in my cheeks. 'I'm sorry. That was rude of me. Please forget I said anything.'

Scully twitched her little nose. It was honestly one of the most adorable things I've ever seen. 'The bunnyboos have a reputation for disregarding laws – and for disrespecting people. And to be honest, it's a well-earned reputation. It's why we're not members of the GU. My family disowned me because I declined to join the pirating business. I came here of my own free will.'

She ran her furry paws down the length of her long ears. 'Of course, I've had to unlearn many of the things I was taught growing up.'

We arrived at a – well, I guess it was a block of flats. It looked a bit like the playing blocks of a giant child. I'd visited Montreal once and stayed near a building called Habitat 67 – a jumble of modular units of all different sizes. Except, where Habitat 67 was a uniform drab grey, this block was every colour under the sun. Under the six suns.

Most of the units weren't even a single colour but were covered in brightly hued artwork of vastly different styles. A few were abstract. Some featured geometric patterns. But about half depicted scenes of people or places.

As Scully led us up a long, sweeping ramp, I asked her, 'What do you mean you had to unlearn things? If you didn't want to be a pirate, wouldn't that be enough?'

Everywhere we walked, we passed people of every shape and size. There were blue lonely robots and multi-coloured peri, a few equidae, various other species I'd met, and loads of people from species I'd never even heard of. I even saw a group of people who were taller than me. This was, by far, the most diverse place I'd ever seen.

I'd almost forgotten I'd asked Scully a question when she finally replied. 'It's very difficult to explain to those lucky enough to come from an inclusive culture. I didn't want to join a pirate crew – that much is true. And I had assumed that my desire to not harm others made me a good person. But when I came here...'

She chuckled. 'This goes back around two decades. I remember I saw someone use her right hand to reach for something. I stood up and sang the song of shunning – and very quickly realised that everyone was staring at me.'

She called back to the others, 'Almost there. You're in this block here.' In a quieter voice she continued, 'You see, where I come from, most people are left-handed. And although we've begun to accept that some people may be born right-handed, many continue to see it as a choice. They say right-handed people violate the natural order of things. Some even argue that freedom means not having to accept that some people are right-handed.'

Scully laid a blue fuzzy paw on my arm as we stopped in front of a bright purple home. 'I'm sorry – this must all seem wildly backwards to someone from an enlightened world.'

I wanted to reply – to explain I was from a planet where evidence and propaganda are presented with equal merit, where the side that makes the most emotive case is deemed to be the winner. Where facts are irrelevant if the majority opinion goes against them.

But before I could compose my thoughts, Scully raised her voice to address the whole group. 'This is it. You can code the lock to respond to you but for now it's on default mode.' She waved her hand over a sensor and the door opened.

Scully held out a paw to Bexley's family. 'After you.'

Alas, Spock ran in first and had a good sniff of the place.

'Er, sorry. She takes her job as security officer seriously.' I made a sheepish face as I turned to Storm, Jean, and Peggy. 'Sorry.'

Jean squeezed my shoulder as she passed. I didn't even have to duck as I followed them in. It dawned on me for the first time that all the doors we'd encountered since landing were tall enough for me.

'It's currently configured in our default layout,' said Scully. 'If you want something else, the walls and furniture can be rearranged to suit your needs. Let me show you how.'

———

Ten minutes later, we left the triad to settle in and agreed to meet up later. Scully offered to take us to a local pub.

Although we were under a dome, the air felt fresh and smelt of herbs and plants I couldn't identify. I held my hand up as we walked. 'It's amazing – it really feels like we're outdoors. There's even a breeze.'

Scully led us in a different direction from the way we'd come. 'Yes, unlike most dome worlds, Lagash's elements aren't hostile to most species – it's only that the atmosphere is too hot. We use the dome to dim the light and cool the air. We could block out more – but it would inhibit the local flora. We have a blend of native and imported plant life.'

This housing estate seemed to go on forever – and every bit of it was more intricately painted than the bit before. The path was wide and smooth. It rose or fell using gentle slopes that people navigating on wheels appeared to have no difficulty with. And again, we passed more species than I'd ever seen in one place.

After about ten minutes, we arrived at a beer garden. We picked a table in the shade of a giant purple ... something. Mushroom? Spock curled up in a ball beneath the table.

No sooner had we made ourselves comfy than Holly announced, 'You said you wished to be alerted immediately if any Hwin representatives arrived at Lagash.'

I glanced around the table. Everyone seemed to be in conversation with their own AIs. 'They're here? Already? What can you tell me?'

'The *Hat* has arrived. Joker has sent an official alert, stating that they have an extradition warrant and will be transporting down to capture the fugitives.'

My hand flew up to my mouth. 'Bloody bollocks.'

Holly wasn't finished. 'Their warrant covers Bexley as well. She's wanted for aiding and abetting in the removal of an infant for purposes deemed abusive under section —'

'What?' I leapt to my feet. 'What are we going to do?'

Bexley got up and ran out the door of the pub.

'The bastards,' I began.

'They're here,' squawked BB.

Aurora's dominant colour was a sort of plum. 'It seems our pursuers have found us. And even if your government is able to protect Storm, Jean, and Peggy – Bexley will be arrested as soon as the *Teapot* tries to leave orbit.'

'We have a plan for this,' said Scully – even as she rose and made to follow Bexley. 'Let's go.'

'I've spoken to Bexley already.' Henry's wheels rolled smoothly as she headed for the exit. 'Can you not move, meatsack?'

I almost knocked my chair over in my haste. Spock did that Scooby-Doo scrabbling-in-place thing. BB hopped down off her perch and clown-marched to the door, her giant taloned feet slowing her down on the flat ground as always.

Holly announced, 'Four Hwin officials have landed on Lagash.'

Scully looked back over her shoulder as she led us away from the pub. 'This does sometimes happen. We have a process in place for dealing with pursuers. Have your friends meet us at the civic centre. I'll call Zippy. My guess is she already knows – but just in case.'

'Hang on.' I struggled to keep up with the others. Henry rolled, Scully hopped, Spock ran, and Aurora floated – all of them faster than BB or I could walk. I trusted their AIs to carry my words to them without any of us slowing down. 'Shouldn't we be trying to get Bexley and her family to go into hiding? If they join us at the civic centre, surely Joker will just arrest them, right? Isn't that the very thing we're trying to avoid?'

'That's a valid concern,' said BB. 'But Scully said they have a process for dealing with these matters. Surely, she wouldn't say that unless she meant it.'

I spun around trying to find where BB's voice was coming from. The thing about universal translators is that everyone's voice is always right in your ear – so you couldn't put any stock in directional hearing.

'Up here, Lem.'

I had to reach out for something to steady myself so I

didn't fall over. I'd never seen BB fly. In fact, I'd not even known for sure whether she could.

She could. And it was quite a sight. She wasn't far above us, just high enough to avoid running into anything. Her wings had to be longer than I was tall. Her body and head feathers were mostly a sunshine yellow but the feathers in her wings were red, blue, and green. With her wings spread, she was as much of a walking rainbow as her spouse. Well, more so, in that Aurora didn't actually walk. Okay, so BB wasn't walking either.

Whatever.

I realised I'd stopped moving to gawp then had to run even harder to catch up with everyone. We arrived at the same time as Bexley and her family. When Scully opened the door, Zippy was there to meet us. BB set down on the ground and walked in just ahead of me.

'Come in; let's get this over with.' Zippy led us across the entrance atrium and into a room on the far side. 'I brought one of my spouses with me. She's an immigration and extradition lawyer.'

As I stepped into the room, I discovered why the doors on Lagash were tall enough to accommodate me. Zippy's spouse's fur was a uniform pale blue-grey. But it was the horn that caught my eye. She had an oil-slick metallic-looking horn. It was *long*. Much longer than I'd expected. Zippy had told us it was almost a metre but I'd assumed that was hyperbole. But what really grabbed me was just how fragile it looked – like an accidental bump would shatter it into a gazillion pieces.

'Hello.' The unicorn spread her arms wide. 'How delightful to meet you gorgeous people – though I wish it were under happier circumstances.' She looked at Spock, her eyes wide. 'Ooh, your fur is positively delicious.'

Spock whimpered and hid behind me. 'No eat Spock.'

The unicorn – Bungle, I decided – clapped her hooves together and laughed. It sounded like a braying donkey. 'Fair enough, my lovely. I promise not to eat you. But only because you asked so nicely.'

Zippy joined her spouse. 'Everyone, take a seat so we can finally get started.' I could never tell whether she was being sarcastic.

We all nodded or tapped hooves or made species-appropriate agreement gestures. Then we all grabbed chairs that looked suitable for our shapes and dragged them over to where Zippy and Bungle stood. Or at least tried to.

Unfortunately, the only chair that looked like it would fit me weighed about as much as I did. And there was no easy way to grip it. I tried dragging it across the room – but all it did was squeak horribly and hold everyone else up. Zippy watched me with one eyebrow cocked.

'You know what – I'll sit on the floor. It'll be fine.' Spock followed me as I joined the others and dropped down onto the floor.

Just as I did so, the door whooshed open and a lonely robot – identical to Henry – rolled in. And no, that's not me passing judgement on anyone's social or emotional status; that's the name of their species.

Zippy looked at the new joiner and lifted her wings; it was the second time I'd seen her use the peri greeting. 'Good of you to join us. I suppose I ought to introduce everyone. You all know by now – or at least you should – Scully and I are part of the oversight committee here on Lagash. I've mentioned my spouse, an immigration and extradition lawyer. And finally, we're joined by our head of law enforcement, who'll explain the plan for this evening.' This time she indicated the robot.

I'd never settled on a name so quickly. Ever. But when the universe gives you a robot cop, you call her Robocop. That's all there is to it.

Jean stepped to the front of the group and introduced herself, her spouses, and the *Teapot* crew.

'Aye, so,' began Henry. No, not Henry; the accent was wrong – *was that Scottish? Why was Robocop Scottish?* I'd never been able to figure out why Holly assigned people the voices it did. 'Our treaty with the GU means that we can't defy the extradi—'

Storm and Peggy both gripped Jean's arms. 'Why did we come here?' shrieked Storm. 'They're going to remove our baby's wings and put us into re-education, and our child will be placed with another family and—'

Jean ran her hooves down the length of Storm's mane. 'Maybe we should let the nice people tell us … whatever they were trying to tell us before you interrupted them, eh?'

Storm quivered and whinnied. Actually whinnied. 'Sure. Fine. Whatever.'

Bungle raised her arms in a gesture that seemed to be intended to placate. 'Oh, sweeties, we've got you. We won't let you go as easily as all that. So don't you worry about going anywhere with them. Unless you want to leave of course – we're not gross. We've granted you provisional citizenship and we stand by that. If those little bitches want you, they'll have to fight us. And, yes, honey, that pun was *fully* intended.'

Much like jokes … puns did not translate. I'd learnt to just go with it.

Bungle winked suggestively. 'But we do still have to abide by our agreement with the GU. If the Hwinners request a hearing, a hearing there shall be.'

Zippy tapped her hooves on the table's edge. 'Most governments – when they discover what a hearing will entail – give up and return home.'

Bexley tossed her mane back over her shoulders. She was

trying not to show it but I could tell she was scared. 'What do you mean, "what a hearing will entail"?'

Zippy ran her hooves over her multi-coloured mane. 'Our hearings are public. By agreeing to one, oppressors are essentially putting their culture on trial. They're asking the GU to weigh in on whether or not their laws are fair and just. Some of our people have been followed here by Hwin representatives. But the Hwin government has *always* declined to pursue the matter.'

Bungle's magnificent horn caught the light as she leant closer to her spouse. 'And when my sexy spouse says *public*, I assure you, she means it. If they opt for a hearing, we'll make sure it will be on every single news site and every station from here to the borders of known space. Escandalo! We know what the peri think of removing an infant's wings.'

'It's depraved!' squawked BB. Standing on a perch directly opposite me, she partially extended her wings. 'Most avian species will be horrified at the idea of surgically removing the wings of infants without their express consent. Even consensual wing removal is a ... well... Bodily autonomy is sacrosanct, obviously.' She raked a taloned hand through her chest feathers.

'See?' Bungle waved a hoof flamboyantly. 'And there are also species in the GU with horns. Let me tell you, they are *not* going to take kindly to the Hwin suggestion that people with horns are lesser beings, if you know what I mean. The fact that unicorns and stags are routinely locked up, that they have lesser and fewer rights than their un-horned counterparts ... honey, that will *not* sit well with other species.'

My hand rose to cover my mouth as I swallowed down a mouthful of bile.

'This is all about as fascinating as a bowl of guacamole

sheep cup,' said Henry. 'But aren't the pluckers going to be here any minute now?'

Bungle waved a hoof dismissively. 'Oh, don't you worry your pretty blue self. The interlopers will be met by a specialist team as soon as they land. They'll be guests of our government until we're ready to see them. And by that I mean —'

'— they won't be permitted to leave the reception centre until the people in this room are ready for them.' Zippy tapped her hooves on the edge of the low table. 'Let's not get ahead of ourselves. There's no reason to assume they'll seek a hearing. It's highly likely that when we present the options to them —'

'They will turn tail and head right back to Hwin,' Bungle finished.

Jean put a hand on both her spouses. 'I fear you may not be aware of how bad things are on Hwin right now. The government has been sliding in an authoritative and intolerant direction for almost a decade – but in the last year or so, things have taken a sharp turn for the worse. Where sometimes there was a policy of "don't ask – don't tell", there's no longer any room for that kind of tacit acceptance.'

Zippy bowed her head. 'I left Hwin when I was a mere four weeks from my parent's pouch. Neither I nor my parents or siblings have been back since. But Bungle...' She faced her blue-furred spouse. 'You should tell your story, sweetie.'

Bungle rested a hoof on her spouse's arm. 'My parents took me to a comfort resort when I was a teen.' She peeled her lips back from her large, flat teeth. 'One of my parents and one of my siblings came to visit me every so often. Seven years ago, my dearest sibling broke me out of that facility. Our parents all disowned her – even the one who had come to visit me. My sibling and I came here together. The Hwin police arrived not long after with warrants for our extradition and arrest. But when told about how the hearings would work ... they opted to leave empty-handed.'

Storm stroked her pouch with one hoof. 'I don't get it. Why had we never heard of this place? And why wasn't this the first place the government looked for us? Why don't they ... I don't know. I'm not even sure what I'm asking.'

Robocop revved her wheels. 'I've just heard from my polis. They're ready to escort the Hwin delegation here. If we give them the go-ahead, they'll be here in nae time at all.'

Zippy tapped her hooves. 'Bungle and Robocop and I will meet their delegation. Scully, would you mind escorting our newest citizens and their guests to their home? Once we've spoken to them, we'll come and discuss further.'

Storm crossed her arms over her chest. 'No, I vote we stay and confront them. They have no right to do this to our family.'

Jean put her hoof on Storm's shoulder. 'Please.'

Bungle bowed her head, her horn glinting as it caught the light. 'Oh, honey, please trust us. I of all people know just how hard this is. But let us handle it for you. You're not alone here.'

Storm stood up, cradling her empty pouch. She chewed her lip for a moment before speaking. 'Fine. I don't like it. My instinct says to stay and fight. But it's not just about me. It's not even just about the three of us.' She put one of her hooves on each of her spouses. 'We'll fight this with all we've got. But let's do it the smart way.'

Peggy sort of snort-neighed but she stood up.

Jean tapped her hooves on the edge of the table as she stood. 'I'm convinced this is the right choice – for us, for our child, and for Bexley. Bexley, do you agree?'

Bexley was already heading for the door. 'Yeah, no, for

sure. I don't like it – but I get it. Part of me hopes they'll opt for the hearing. Because this will never really be over until the laws are changed. That's the only way we can actually win this thing.'

I could tell Bexley wasn't finished – but Scully managed to sneak into the conversation when Bexley paused for breath. 'If you're all ready? We ought to get away before the Hwin delegation arrives.'

We all followed her as she hopped back outside under the dome. The housing estate was a few streets over, rising above most of the other buildings in the area.

The family's new home had been transformed. Most of the interior walls and doors were gone. The centre of the flat was set up as a lounge.

Storm paced, tapping frantically at her tablet, while the rest of us got seated. 'Quark sent us a link to a news bulletin. She's worried about us. It better not have been her who turned us in to the authorities. I'll bet it was her, you know? I've never trusted—'

Jean stroked Storm's mane. 'It wasn't Quark, sweetheart.'

Peggy took the tablet from Storm's hooves. 'Put the bulletin on already. The suspense is killing me.'

An outer wall vanished as the room appeared to extend several metres.

A stage appeared with several equidae on it. One spoke directly to the camera. 'Good evening and welcome to *Debate Hour*. I'm joined tonight by a Traditional Party politician from global parliament' – she gestured towards a dour-faced person with a pale blue mane – 'a politician from the Separatist Party, a social worker who specialises in children with the disorder, and finally a parent with one of the saddest stories I've ever heard.'

We all fell silent as the host approached the last person she'd introduced. 'I understand your child had the defect, yes?'

The person – a short, plump equidae with a pink mane – tapped her hooves. 'Yes, we had to get the surgery done on my sweet little baby to correct the defect. After that, everything seemed fine for a few years. But then...' She whimpered noisily. 'Her tail started to grow in.'

The host raised a hoof to her mouth. 'Now, when you say "her tail", you don't mean an ordinary hair-based tail, do you? You mean she had the affliction, don't you?'

The young parent sobbed as she tapped her hooves again. 'Yeah. She did. And we had that removed as well. Even got her a nice wigtail. We thought she was finally going to be normal after that.'

She pulled a hanky from her holster and dabbed her eyes. 'But when she hit puberty, she began clawing at her face like an animal. It was horrible – she bled everywhere. And that's when I knew.' She wailed uncontrollably.

There was an audible gasp from the other members of the panel. Peggy threw something at the holo-scene. Whatever it was passed right through the crying parent's face.

'This is garbage. They're debating people's right to exist and they don't even have the decency to include one of us in their debate.'

Jean put her arms around Peggy as she handed the tablet to Bexley. 'Shut it off, would you?'

Bexley's breath was hot on my face. 'Lem! Wake up! Are you dreaming again? What are we going to do?'

I rubbed the sleep from my eyes. 'Don't wanna. Not even pizza day.' The sun was way too bright. Correction: the *suns* were way too bright. A hasty glance through my eyelashes out the hotel room's window showed three of them in view. I pinched my eyes shut again.

Bexley shook my shoulder. 'I don't know if they'll have pizza available at the breakfast bar. But I'm kinda panicking here. I need your help. You're always so calm in a crisis.'

I opened one eye. My mind began to catch up with my body. 'Sorry. What?' I raised a hand to block the light. 'Actually, can you pull the curtains shut?'

The bed bounced as she jumped off. 'Okay.' She paced the room as the window turned mostly opaque. The ambient light dimmed to a more bearable level.

I pushed myself to a sitting position. 'Thank you. Sorry.' I stretched my arms. 'Something happened, I take it?'

Bexley clutched at her mane, rubbing her face. 'They're going ahead with the hearing. They've got a stack of arrest warrants – it's not just us. They've got warrants and extradition orders for every single unicorn and pegasus and possum and stag and everyone and all their parents too. And Bungle's sibling and a few other people as well. Everyone who left in the last, like, two decades or something. Practically the entire equidae population on Lagash is affected. Thousands of people. They were all so nice to us and look what we've caused. Everything's crashing down around them and it's all our fault and—'

'Hey.' I clambered off the bed and wrapped my arms around her. 'Hey, hey hey. This colony was established specifically because they wanted to make a home for people like your family. Almost everyone on this planet – well, moon – has something like this hanging over them. You didn't bring this on them and you're not fighting it alone.'

Bexley's shoulders fell. 'But we brought the Hwin cops here. It's our fault.'

I shrugged helplessly. 'I mean, okay, sort of. But not really.'

She looked up at me, eyes glistening. 'I don't know if you missed the part where they literally followed us here.'

Spock got off the bed and made her way to the bathroom.

I smacked my forehead to get the thoughts moving. 'Yeah, that's true. But everyone who's here came to escape something. And there are a lot of equidae here. What did Zippy tell us? A couple thousand, I think. And every single one of them is here because of the injustice on Hwin. The fact that your family was the one who finally tipped the government over the edge…'

I scrunched up my face as I struggled to find the right words for what I meant. 'In the end, this isn't about you or your semi-sibling or Storm or your step-dads. It's about *all* equidae. It's about your right to live your life as your authentic selves. That's what Lagash is all about. Scully and her right-handed friends. Henry and Robocop and their right to not be subjugated by ... I don't know whoever created them.'

I sat down on the edge of the bed. 'There are a lot of people on Earth who'd love to find a society as inclusive as this one. People who are desperate for a better life – who just want to be themselves. But nothing stays as tolerant and welcoming as Lagash without hard work. I'd wager all the money in my account that pretty much everyone here has known this was coming. They're ready for this. This isn't just about your family.'

I took a deep breath. 'I mean, it *is* about your family. Obviously, it's about you.'

I let my head fall into my hands. 'When I was on Earth, there were these powerful groups who oppressed transgender people. Well, I mean, they oppressed all sorts of minority and marginalised groups. But anyway. Of course, it was about me. But it was never *just* about me. Even when I was the one being shouted at for using the "wrong" toilet or when someone accused me of being a predator or a groomer or a paedophile or whatever. It was never about me. And this isn't about you. Everyone here is in it together.'

My empty stomach was flip-flopping inside me. I wished I could explain myself better.

Bexley threw herself face down on the bed and sobbed. Spock returned from the loo and climbed up on the bed, nuzzling into her.

'But that's what I mean,' wailed Bexley. 'If we lose, it isn't just us. Half the equidae on Lagash will either be subjected to unnecessary surgery or chucked into comfort resorts. The other half will go for "re-education".'

She didn't use rabbit ears around the last word – but she

must have used some kind of equivalent because I could hear them in the emphasis the AI gave the word.

Most of the time in the GU, when people were found guilty of a crime, they were fined or had to undergo re-education and rehabilitation. Sometimes both. It had always seemed like a very mature and sensible way of dealing with crime.

For the first time, I saw how it could be used for ill. I shook my head to clear it. 'It'll be okay.'

'You can't know that,' Bexley whispered.

'You're right. I can't. But we'll face it together.' I gave her a quick squeeze before standing up and stretching.

———

It didn't take me long to get dressed and ready. 'Let's go grab some breakfast.'

Spock wagged her tail and ran to the door. 'Feed Spock?'

Bexley, still lying on her stomach, released a slow breath as she stood up. 'Yeah. Let's go. And of course we'll feed you, silly. We're all going to eat.'

When the hotel room door slid aside, I felt like I'd been punched in the gut. On the opposite side of the hall, Joker stood waiting.

Beneath her long red mane, her shield of office glinted as it caught the light. 'Good morning.' She batted her long eyelashes and smiled cordially.

I scowled at her. 'You're not allowed to be here.'

'Yeah.' Bexley stabbed a hoof in Joker's direction. 'We talked to Bungle – the law says you're not allowed to arrest us before the hearing as long as we remain on Lagash. We know our rights. You can't touch us.'

Joker pushed off the wall and studied Bexley. 'You

trusted the word of a unicorn?' She snorted. 'Surely you know better than that. And anyway, I'm not touching you. I'm here to help.'

The muscles along Bexley's long nose started twitching. My fingernails bit into my palms.

'We can help each other, you know. Your semi-sibling,' Joker continued. 'You seem like a reasonable person, Bexley. Surely you don't want to see her raised in this sinful place. With the defect uncorrected. You don't want that kind of life for her, do you?'

My gut twisted and clenched. 'Leave her alone. She's not going to sell her parents out to you, you … you … menace. The hearing will show your bigotry for what it is. Storm and the others will stay here and bring up their baby, free of hate.'

Joker tossed her mane back over her shoulder. 'Actually, I'm confident the hearing will yield the correct result. This planet stands in open defiance of science. Now, that might be fine for *aliens*…' She cast a sideways glance at me. 'But all knowledge-fearing areions—'

'Stop using that word,' Bexley bellowed. 'It's ableist.' She stamped her hoof on the floor.

Joker ran a hoof down her mane. 'Think about what I said. I can help you.' With that, she turned and sauntered away.

Bexley's nostrils flared.

'Come on.' I put my arm around her. She let me guide her in the opposite direction from the one Joker had gone. 'Let's get some breakfast.'

Bexley snorted as we walked. 'I just thought of another of her jokes. Who's yellow and boring? And then the answer is — Holy crap! That joke is totally otherphobic – I don't know why I never thought of it before. It's really gross.'

She tilted her head, lips moving as she recited jokes to

herself the whole way down to the hotel's dining room. 'You know what? Now that I think of it, most of her jokes are at the expense of people who are different in some way.'

I'd dealt with so much othering for so long. But it didn't prepare me for this. Despite all my own experience of being someone else's punchline or punching bag, I still didn't know how to help. 'I'm sorry.'

'Okay, I'll tell you another joke. Not one of hers. An actual, proper, funny joke. What's black and white?'

I grinned sadly as we picked a table and sat down. 'I don't know, Bex. What's black and white?'

'Oxidative phosphorylation.'

———

Neither the Hwin government nor Lagash's oversight committee wanted this whole affair dragged out any longer than strictly necessary, so the hearing was set for the following week. And we had our work cut out for us getting ready. In the meantime, BB re-implanted the foetus from Henry's incubator to Storm's pouch.

Once she woke after the re-implantation procedure, she set to work contacting people friendly to our cause. As a journalist, Storm had connections across the galaxy – and her connections had connections. Lagash became the galactic news story of the moment. Every news outlet was covering the hearing. Experts on every side were weighing in.

The parent we'd seen on the current affairs show sobbed her way through an endless series of interviews.

Everyone wanted to come to Lagash to cover the hearing. Journalists, bloggers, activists, social media influencers – because, yes, apparently they were a thing in the GU too. Droves of people descended on the little colony. At least virtually. Thanks to the colony's strict immigration policies, only accredited journalists could set foot on Lagash. But that didn't stop them from trying … and not every journalist was ethical.

I looked at my phone screen and then up at Bungle. 'Bexley just messaged. She and her family are running a bit late. They should be here in about a quarter of an hour or so.' My throat constricted as my mind created increasingly implausible reasons for their delay.

Bungle nodded, her horn catching the light as it dipped. 'Well then, I suppose we should get this party started. They'll join as soon as they can and we'll catch them up on the bits they've missed.'

Since the start of the week, we'd begun each day with a meeting in the conference room at the civic centre.

Zippy, Scully, and Robocop joined the meetings, though their days were filled with the running of the colony. The rest of us – Bungle, Bexley's family, and the *Teapot* crew – were all working flat out to get ready for the hearing.

Robocop blinked into existence at the edge of the table. 'Morning, all. Sorry I cannae attend in person today. My team and I are working around the clock, trying to keep unauthorised individuals offa Lagash. We been called out overnight to come rescue another batch.'

'Who are they?' asked Zippy. 'Unaccredited journalists? Equidae activists? Agitators?'

Robocop extended two appendages and clapped them together. 'As near as I can tell, these chuckleheads are professional spectators. Figured they'd come up with a brilliant plan, aye. Two dozen of them landed in a getoff about ten kilometres from the colony. Uh course, these divs put e'en less thought into getting from there to here. They had goggles and parasols – but had nae counted on the sixty-degree temperatures. The roasters made it almost a kilometre before they needed rescuing.'

'You'd think they'd learn,' said Scully. 'Everyone caught trying to sneak in finds herself back on her ship in short order.'

'Aye, well, I'm sure some do learn. Not the bampots, though,' griped Robocop. 'We're giving this lot emergency medical aid. We'll send them packing as soon as they're well enough to travel.'

She extended a jointed arm and held it up in what I'd interpret as a 'hold on' gesture. After a moment, she continued. 'The officers stationed at Storm's home just foiled an attack. Pair of bawbags casing the place. They had tranqs and grab bags – both illegal, of course.'

I leapt up, tripping over my chair. 'Bexley!' Someone had tossed a grab bag over my head once. Not only could I not see, but the bag had also paralysed me. When you're caught in one, you can breathe and blink but not resist.

'Sit down, cheesecake.' Henry extruded a long flat implement and slowly lowered it. 'Robocop said her officers caught them before they tried anything. Besides, what were you going to do – run over there and get kidnapped instead?'

Bungle gently placed a hoof on my arm. 'We've all got our tasks to do, sweetie. Yours is here. I admire your devotion to your mate but we need you here. We all need to do our part prepping for this hearing.'

She turned back to the Robocop. 'Thanks for the update, my lovely. You and your team are all doing brilliantly. Ta ta for now.' Bungle tapped daintily at her tablet and Robocop blinked out of existence.

'Now. On to the plan for today.' She looked up at the wall, where the schedule I'd drawn up for everyone's time was projected. 'The family has another interview lined up this afternoon. This one's with the GBC. It's not going to be easy-breezy. Storm's prepped them for some tough questions. But it should run more smoothly than the one yesterday with those dreadful people at POX News.'

The door slid open and Bexley and her family bustled in. I ran and threw my arms around her. 'We just heard! Are you okay? What happened?'

Spock pressed her nose into Bexley's side. 'Bexley okay.'

Bexley looked at Storm and then back at me. 'Yeah, it's all a bit of a mess. She only just called. I haven't spoken to her in a few months and I really thought she'd be on our side in all this and— Wait, how did you hear?'

I scratched my head. 'What? We heard from Robocop.'

Bexley took a step away from me. 'How the hell did Robocop find out?'

'It was one of her team that intercepted them,' I said.

'What?'

'What?'

Bexley and I stared at one another for a few moments.

Bungle looked at us both. 'My lovelies, I'm going to suggest you're not talking about the same event.'

'Perhaps if you'd all care to join us we can try to get this meeting back on track,' added Zippy.

'Yeah, no, sorry,' said Bexley as she and her parents took their seats. Spock and I returned to our places as well.

Bungle ran her hoof down her long mane. 'Bexley, why don't you tell us what happened this morning?'

Bexley mirrored Bungle's body language, smoothing her own mane. 'Oh, yeah, sure. So you know how we've all been getting loads of unwanted calls, right? I mean, mainly my dad, but also all of us. We've had people trying to speak to us at all hours of the day and night. See, among those people are all my other dads. They've been calling, like, nonstop every day since the news broke.'

Storm tapped her hooves on the edge of the table. 'I may be at the centre of the media storm, but everyone around me is affected in one way or another. All my former spouses – especially Bexley's other dads – are being hounded and chased for comment. Bexley and I have both had angry calls from all of them.'

'They want Dad to call the whole thing off,' said Bexley. 'All of them. Anyways, this morning as we were on our way here, my dad called. The one with the pink hair, I mean. I tried to decline the call but she just kept trying over and over and anyways eventually I answered and she just started shouting at me. She said this was all my fault and—' She dropped her head to the table and cried.

My tummy felt like a lead weight. I could tell Bexley thought that some of her dads blamed her. I had no idea whether they actually did – only that Bexley thought so. But how could any parent treat her child that way? My dad died before I started presenting in a more feminine way but I felt confident he would have accepted me so long as I was true to myself and hurting no one.

Stretching a hand across the table, I whispered, 'I'm so sorry.'

Bungle ran a hoof over her long blue mane. 'Lem, dear, we need you to continue your work on scheduling. Our list of witnesses still needs work. So far, we've got some great examples of healthy, happy, well-adjusted skelediverse equidae. But now let's focus on finding our own experts to rebut their experts.'

I took a sip of my lukewarm helbru. I rolled the floral flavours around on my tongue before swallowing. 'But surely the very existence of these people' – I waved a hand at the faces on my tablet – 'disproves their experts.'

Zippy raised her arms above her head and arched her back, stretching out her powerful muscles. 'It's a good start. The people selected so far all tell compelling stories. But that's all they are – stories. Anecdotes. We need more – specifically about unmolested skeledivergents. Average lifespans. Disease rates. Surgical procedures. Instances of broken bones. Rates of criminal behaviour. We need facts and evidence. Data. *Irrefutable* data.'

A sharp crack made me jump – Storm slamming her hooves down on the table. 'We're working on it! Do you have any idea how hard it is to find research that doesn't assume skelediversity is anything other than a vulgar throwback?'

Peggy ran a hoof down Storm's silver-white mane. 'People take these myths as given. When I first started researching, I was coming at it from a perspective of wanting to improve the quality of life for those few pegasuses who *couldn't* have the surgery – you know, for medical or religious reasons. When I approached various institutions about undertaking my research, I was met with derision. Why would I want to help regressives and mediphobes?'

Peggy shuddered. 'Securing grants and approval to conduct my research was so much harder than it should have been. And even once I'd secured the funding, I hit roadblock after roadblock. I faced ethical challenges. Journals declined to publish or even consider my work for review. Department heads were unsupportive. Research assistants and technologists refused to work with me. One agreed to but then her family talked her out of it, convincing her that her career would … suffer…' She seemed to get lost in thought at that point.

Jean leant against Peggy's shoulder. 'Hardly anyone is doing research that would potentially show there's nothing inherently inferior about skeledivergent people,' Jean said. 'It's been standard practice for pegasuses to have their wings removed at emergence for so long that there's no reliable research on the health of those who keep them. There are no independently verified studies into co-morbidities. The religious groups that don't allow the surgery are small. The infants who can't have the procedure for medical reasons... Well, for the most part, what happens is surgeons attempt the excision and the infants die. The number of babies who survive a failed attempt is vanishingly small. The only reliable studies into skeledivergent health have been performed here on Lagash. The timeline is short and the numbers are small.'

Peggy stood and ran from the room. Glancing back over her shoulder, she called out, 'I'm going to call that technician. If she hasn't carried on with her research independently she may at least know others who've done so.'

'Okay, well then,' Bungle turned to BB and then Henry, 'that's where you come in, my lovelies. We need you to keep poring through the medical and scientific journals to find us both experts and data. The reports coming out of Hwin are largely skewed by their flawed assumptions, so we're looking for the jewels amongst the dross.'

Bungle addressed Aurora. 'And you, you sparkling person... You and I will be interviewing potential witnesses to determine their suitability. And lastly, that brings us to you, gorgeous.' She reached a hoof out and booped Spock's snoot. 'Your task is to keep us all safe. You'll accompany BB and me to our meetings with witnesses. And between meetings, you'll guard the office here to keep us safe from any hostile activities.'

'Spock protect.'

## 15 / VIOLET, HORTA, FERN,
## AND BEES

The GU had assembled a panel of ... well, the best word would probably be magistrates. Not judges. Not lawyers. At least, I didn't think so. They were sort of like a professional jury: people who travelled around the galaxy listening to cases and making decisions.

There were four of them on the panel. Violet, the large purple person we'd met on Deep Space Five, was joined by a giant rock-like horta, and two people whose species I didn't recognise.

Two sets of people stood facing the magistrates. On the left, Zippy, Bungle, Scully, and Robocop were ready to argue our case. On the right, there were four equidae. I didn't recognise most of them – but the figure on the end had a long, lustrous ginger mane and wore a periwinkle vest.

Joker.

Shuddering, I took my seat in the first row of the audience. Except that makes it sound like I had a chair. I did not. I sat on the floor like everyone else. Well, not quite everyone. Peri stood on perches around the edges of the room. And some people – like Aurora and Henry – didn't sit. Whatever.

We arranged ourselves and sat, stood, or hovered in accordance with our respective biologies.

Spock lay down on one side of me. Bexley sat on the other. Beyond her was her family.

The horta addressed the room. 'Good morning, citizens of both the GU and Lagash colony, as well as other friends. We're gathered here today to determine whether certain specific Hwin laws violate the Galactic Union Charter of Rights and Freedoms.'

I'd almost forgotten how small and dainty Violet's voice was. 'For those of you who have not previously attended a hearing of this sort, please allow me to give you a quick rundown of what to expect. We'll open with prepared speeches. Each side will have nine and a half minutes to make their case. After that, we'll hear witness testimony. Both the petitioners and the challengers have provided a list of people who will speak in support of their cases. Once each witness has given her testimony, the petitioners and the challengers will each have twelve minutes to question them.'

The person next to the horta – who looked like a pink fern – picked up the thread. 'Once we have heard from all the witnesses, the petitioners and the challengers will each be accorded thirteen and a third minutes to present their closing arguments. Then my colleagues and I will retire to discuss what we've observed.'

The final magistrate resembled a swarm of bees. 'On rare occasions, we may ask one or more witnesses to return to answer questions posed by us. However, normally, we're able to render a decision after debating amongst ourselves. In most cases, our verdict will represent a compromise between what the petitioners and the challengers want. Any questions from the petitioners?'

One member of the Hwin delegation stood briefly. 'No, tiz.'

The bees collectively pivoted towards the left. My left. Her right. Their right. Whatever. 'Any questions from the challengers?'

Bungle also stood to reply. 'No, tiz.'

Fern's leaves fluttered as if caught by a gentle breeze. 'Then we'll begin. Petitioners, you have nine and a half minutes.'

The same equidae rose for a second time. 'Thank you, tizzes. I understand that areion ways' – I bristled at the use of the outdated term and several others in the room appeared to shiver – 'may appear unusual to members of other species. It's possible they may even seem cruel to the uneducated. But I assure the magistrates, the people present in the audience today, and those watching a recording of these proceedings … nothing could be further from the truth.'

She stepped away from her chair and looked around the room. 'The correction of the defect has been presented recently as an unnecessary procedure on an unconsenting infant.' She touched a hoof to her chest. 'The challengers would have you believe that we do this because we don't love our children. Because we don't want them to grow to be healthy adults. Because we are cruel.'

She made smiling eye contact with people all around the room as she spoke. 'The truth is, we love our children more than other species could possibly understand.' Nice. Not remotely insulting to everyone in the room or anything. 'It is precisely because of our deep, selfless love that we are prepared to do what must be done for our children. When a foetus has the defect, we don't revel in the opportunity to disfigure her, whatever Storm and her family might tell you.

When a child develops the disorder, we grieve for her – for the person she'll never be.'

I felt sick.

Closing her eyes for a moment, she pursed her lips. 'I'll make a confession. My third child developed the disorder – or unicornism to give it its proper name. None of you can understand what that's like. Up to a certain point, she developed normally. She was a typical child. Her intelligence, development, and behaviour had seemed perfectly normal.'

She flared her nostrils and breathed out noisily. 'But one day, everything changed. She became moody and irritable. Her ability to think coherently fell away. Over a period of weeks, my beloved child regressed. I mourned her. My spouses and I sought out the best comfort resort on the continent and spared no expense in taking her there. The whole family accompanied her so we could have a proper goodbye. The sounds she made when she realised what was happening—'

She bit off her words. 'It hurt me more than it hurt her; I can tell you that for certain.' *I bet it didn't.* 'This was my child. I'd watched her grow in my spouse's pouch. I'd fed her at my breast. I'd changed her nappies. I'd taught her to roll hay. And then I left her behind.'

Tears rolled freely down her sanctimonious face. I glanced around the room and saw Bexley and her family grinding their teeth.

The speaker took a moment to sniffle and cry for the audience while my blood boiled inside me. 'Those of you who've never raised a child with special needs don't understand what it's like. Our struggles are real. Try and imagine how it is for us. How much patience, discipline, and love we gift to a child who doesn't understand those things. A child who can never return them.'

I bit back the desire to run across the room and punch her. It wasn't until I tasted blood that I realised how hard I'd bitten myself.

'Over the next few days, you'll hear from parents like me. But you'll also hear from scientists and experts. The choice before this tribunal is a simple one: do we, as loving parents, have the right to do what's best for our children? Having a child afflicted with the disorder, it's true, does mean surrendering that child to the state – but the homes they go to are staffed with teams of people who are equipped to meet their needs. As part of this hearing, you'll visit some of those facilities and see how lovely they are. And as for the defect, the procedure to correct it is simple, painless, and routine.'

The room swam around me. I didn't know how much more of this I could take.

'This hearing will show you the necessity and justness of our ways. And at the end of the week, honourable tizzes, I know you'll vote to uphold our laws.'

The smug prick finally resumed her seat.

Scully stood and gave a speech. A really good speech. All about, well, about all the stuff we'd been discussing for the past few weeks, ever since Storm first called us.

But the testimonials... Some of them broke my heart. Others made me feel kind of murder-y.

One of the first witnesses that day was the tiniest equidae I'd ever seen. Not that she was a child – just a very petite adult. 'Good morning. My name is [no frame of reference]. I'm a carpenter and a citizen of Lagash.'

Hearing someone introduce herself using her actual name jarred me. But I supposed most people watching or listening to the hearing wouldn't be using translators – or at least they wouldn't do so when an equidae was speaking.

'I've lived here for seven and a half years, ever since...'

Her voice faltered for a moment but she pressed on. 'When my spouses and I were expecting a baby, we were told the embryo had the defect. Like most equidae, we didn't think much of it at the time. We knew she'd have to have the procedure when she was born – but we weren't worried.'

Looking at the floor, she continued. 'We should've worried. When our baby was born, the doctors took her away to remove her wings. Only they returned empty-handed. Our baby – my baby – didn't survive the procedure. Afterwards, my spouses and I grieved. We were all sad ... but in time, they recovered. I couldn't. I couldn't get past it. And so I started to research. When I learnt that the procedure might not actually be necessary, I was furious.'

She took a sip of water. 'I was unable to let it go. My spouses were supportive at first but when they started talking about trying again, I left them. I continued my research and eventually discovered Lagash. I left everything and everyone I'd ever known and came here on my own.'

At the end of her speech, Joker got up and sauntered over to her and rested her arm casually on the desk between them. She turned and cast another of her oh-so-charming smiles around the room. 'Thank you for your testimony, citizen. Tell me, if you can, what percentage of the procedures are successful?'

It was clear the witness had done her homework. In fact, I knew she had because we'd anticipated this question. She held her head high. 'Current estimates put the figure at one in every 423 infants die in this completely unnecessary surgery.'

Joker tapped her hooves on the desk. 'So, you admit that the procedure is successful in 99.8 per cent of cases?'

The proceedings carried on like that. Volleying back and forth.

A slender pale beige equidae took the stand. 'Good day,

esteemed magistrates and audience members. My name is [no frame of reference] and I am an orthopaedic researcher at the University of [no frame of reference] on Hwin. My area of speciality is pegacism – or *the defect* in common parlance. For forty years, I've studied people with symptoms of pegacism at all levels of development – mainly neonates but not excluding adolescents and even a few adults. I am the foremost expert in the field – I don't say that as a boast but as a simple state-ment of fact. There is no one alive who knows more about pegacism than I do.'

Her nostrils flared as she took a deep breath. 'The proce-dure to correct the defect is simple, humane, and painless.'

Joker's back muscles twitched – clenching and releas-ing – at that statement, causing her thin gilet to flutter. It was quick. If I'd not been looking her way at that precise moment, I'd have missed it entirely.

The scientist continued. 'The few unaltered adolescents and adults I've studied have had statistically significantly reduced quality of life and poorer health outcomes than the average person. They suffer from repeated infections and spinal malformations, as well as certain malignancies and neoplasms. The wings are the site of chronic pain and a source of endless irritation and inflammation. For reasons that aren't clear to us, they also have lower median incomes, shorter life expectancy, and reduced numbers of sexual partners.'

*Gee, I can't imagine why being a social pariah would lead to lower earnings or a less fulfilled life.*

When the scientist's testimony concluded, Zippy stood up to question her. She normally used the peri habit of raising her wings a few centimetres as a greeting. But this time she didn't stop there. She spread her wings up and out – not all the way but far enough to see them clearly. Each one was more than a metre in length. Unlike peri wings, they weren't feathered. They were more like dragonfly wings; an iridescent gossamer film stretched across the fine, delicate bones. They caught the light from the windows and shone in every colour imaginable. She held them for a few moments and then folded them back in.

The scientist's mouth dropped open but she slammed it shut. A jealous look flitted across her face. I wasn't sure whether she wanted to be Zippy – or to cut her open and study her.

'Tell me, doctor,' said Zippy. 'Were you born a pegasus?'

The scientist's nostrils flared. 'That ... that's none of your business. It's a very personal question.'

Zippy flicked her head, setting her short rainbow-hued mane aquiver. 'I don't know, doctor. You profess to be the galaxy's greatest expert in being a pegasus. I have lived almost forty-seven years *as* a pegasus – longer even than you've studied people like me. So, tell me, doctor, are you a pegasus? Do you know what it feels like to spread your wings? To fly? Do you know how the stumps of a botched removal burn? Come on, doctor. Surely if you're an expert in all things pegasus, you must at least know the emotional and physical scars of having your wings removed?'

Once again, I noticed Joker bristling at Zippy's remarks. I wondered if she had a skeledivergent child.

The scientist crossed her arms over her chest. 'I was not born with pegacism.'

Zippy mirrored the scientist's body language. 'And yet you assert you know more about being a pegasus than I do?'

The scientist's ears pivoted like little satellite dishes. 'Of course not. That would be an absurd assertion. I don't know what it is to be you any more than I know what it is to be a peri or a horta. But I am an expert in how pegacism affects the areion musculoskeletal system and the immune system.'

Zippy chuckled. 'Technically speaking, I do not have an areion skeleton – because, by its very definition, the word areion denotes a skeletypical equidae. And it may surprise you to know that I'm a bit of an expert in having a pegasus musculoskeletal system.'

Before continuing, Zippy paused and took a drink from a water glass on the table. 'I'd like you to tell me more about this chronic pain and endless irritation and inflammation.'

The scientist bristled. 'Individuals affected by pegacism are eight per cent more likely to report back pain than skeletypical individuals. Also, we have extensive records of people experiencing inflammation and irritation local to the site of the excision.'

Zippy chewed her lips. 'Hmm. So, in your *expert* opinion, the health problems associated with pegacism stem more from the removal of the wings than from the wings themselves. Is that correct?'

The scientist spluttered. 'Well, that's hardly a fair comparison. Almost ninety-nine per cent of people with pegacism have their wings removed at birth.'

Zippy smirked as she looked around the room. Fair to say she'd won that round.

———

The first day's session ended with the parent we'd seen on the public affairs show, appearing by hologram. And just like her TV appearance, she blubbed all the way through her testimony.

'I believe the universe gave me this child for a reason. I've asked myself so often what that reason could be.' *Sob*. 'But now I know. All my struggles have been so that I can show the galaxy how vital our Hwin strategies for dealing with these people are. I suppose, if you come from a lawless society where special needs people are allowed to wreak havoc on society, our laws may seem strict…'

My eyes rolled so hard I worried my retinas would detach. I tuned her out after that.

A few minutes later, people around me were pulling themselves to an upright position. We'd made it through the first day of the hearing.

There were dozens of witnesses over the next few days: some experts in their fields and others who spoke from personal experience. Most of their testimonies blended into one another in my mind but a few stuck with me.

Zippy took the stand on the second day. Her rainbow mane looked spikier than normal. 'Good morning. My name is Zippy. I'm part of the oversight committee here on Lagash. Specifically, my role is Head of Intake and Citizenship. I was born on Hwin and I am a pegasus.' She lifted her wings a bit – just enough so they were visible to the cameras and the people facing her. 'On the day of my birth, my parents did as good equidae have done for centuries – they handed me over for the procedure. But things did not go to plan.'

Zippy turned to face the magistrates directly. 'May I call one of my spouses over to assist me in a brief demonstration?'

The magistrates leant into one another and whispered amongst themselves for a few seconds.

'We have no objections,' said Fern. 'You may proceed.'

'Thank you,' said Zippy.

Bungle left the table where counsel for our side sat. Zippy

extended her left wing while simultaneously twisting it forwards, wrapping it around herself like a cape.

Zippy turned her back to the room and faced the wall. 'If you look here, just at the base of my wing, you'll see extensive scar tissue.' As she spoke, Bungle gestured to the area in question. 'Also, it does this.' Bungle reached out and gently pried the base of the wing – it pulled away at an odd angle. Her wing had been partially torn from her torso.

'With Bungle's help, I can hold this pose for a while if anyone would like to get a closer look. Of course, we will also submit holographs of the injuries so the magistrates can review them at their convenience.' She turned back to face Bungle and the room. 'Thank you.'

Bungle touched Zippy's shoulder gently then returned to her seat at the desk.

Zippy continued her testimony. 'The surgeon began cutting my wing only to discover my pulmonary artery is atypically placed. If she had continued, she'd have severed the artery and I would have bled out. Thankfully, she spotted the problem in time and stopped the surgery. She left my wings intact. My parents brought me here and I grew up as my true self. Thanks to the damage from the aborted procedure, I am unable to fly – but at least I'm alive. And intact.'

The next witness that stands out in my mind was a psychiatrist who worked in the comfort resorts.

She smiled sweetly and wore a jaunty patterned scarf at her throat. 'I work with people suffering from the disorder – what you would call unicornism – on a daily basis.' Her face contorted into a sneer. 'My work has me travelling between comfort resorts. I love my patients and they love me. But they are not people – not in the way we tend to think of the word. Or rather, they're not *whole* people.'

Silently, I counted primes. *Two, three, five, seven, eleven, thir-*

*teen*. Deep breath. *Seventeen, nineteen, twenty-three, twenty-nine, thirty-one, thirty-seven.* I was practically screaming the numbers in my mind.

She coughed and touched her scarf. 'I also train others in my field and I regularly remind them of that fact. We start pretty much from scratch when we work with people afflicted with the disorder. They are people in the physical sense – they have a nose and a mouth and a mane. But not in the psychological sense. In order to help them, we must first construct the person.'

Bile rushed into my mouth. I tried to swallow but my muscles just wouldn't co-operate. On my left, Bexley clutched my hand and squeezed until I accidentally cried out, dribbling bile into my other hand. I pulled a tissue from my pocket and wiped it off.

The sweet little old person who wanted to lock Bexley, and everyone like her, into an institution continued. 'In the vast majority of cases, those with the disorder never truly become people in their own right. As they are unable to look after themselves, we provide supportive, loving, lifelong care. We remove the burden from the families and spread the cost across the taxpayers – offset of course by menial tasks they perform for the betterment of society. The comfort resorts are wonderful places – far better than anything the residents would be able to maintain for themselves.'

I covered my mouth with my hand and tried to breathe out my rage.

'In fact,' she continued, 'left to their own devices, most people with the disorder would simply die of malnutrition or infection. Those of you who aren't areion simply can't understand what they're like.'

I leapt up and ran from the room, barely making it to the hall before I lost my lunch into the nearest rubbish bin. When the last of what I'd eaten had purged itself, I fell to the floor, spent. Bexley and Spock had followed me out.

Spock gave my face a good long sniff and then sat down by my side. 'Be okay, Lem.'

Bexley put a hoof on my shoulder. 'Are you all right? Your body rejected the food you ate – was there something wrong with it?'

A chill came over me as I looked up at her. 'Did you not hear what she said?' I glanced around and lowered my voice. 'She was talking about you and everyone like you.'

'Oh, that.' Bexley's nostrils flared. 'Yeah, no, sorry. I've just … I guess … huh. You know, until Bungle, I'd never known another unicorn. I mean, not one who wasn't locked up and drugged. But she seems all right, doesn't she?'

I hauled myself to my feet. 'Can we step outside for a bit – get some fresh air? Is that okay? And yeah, Bungle is brilliant.'

'Of course.' I could feel the tears welling in my eyes.

As we headed for the exit, Bexley was silent. Once we got outside, she said, 'I wonder… What if it's not true at all? What if unicorns really are just ordinary people who happen to look a bit different and that's all?'

Putting my arm around my best friend, I replied, 'There's nothing wrong with you. There never has been. It's society that's broken, not you.'

We missed Bungle's cross-examination of the shrink – though I've seen the recording and it was everything she deserved.

———

There was another witness for the petitioner. She was a plump mauve equidae who attended in person. Her shoulders quivered as she took the stand. She had a spiky, broom-like mane. It took me a minute to figure out why she was so famil- iar. In fact, it was her voice that triggered my memory in the end. She was the surgeon we'd met when Storm was in the fertility clinic back on Hwin.

My stomach leapt inside me. I had liked her.

Once she was in position, she swallowed and glanced at the petitioners at their desk. 'Good morning. My name is [no frame of reference] and I am an orthopaedic surgeon at the Happy Families Clinic in [no frame of reference] on Hwin. And I...' She stole another glance at the petitioners and licked her lips before continuing. 'And I hereby make a formal request for residency on Lagash.'

The courtroom burst into a chaotic whirlwind of overlap- ping shouts and wild gesticulations. Holly couldn't interpret all of it – or maybe it could have but knew I wouldn't be able to follow. I had no idea who was saying what to whom.

The bees coalesced tighter together. 'In light of this devel- opment, we're going to take an early break,' they said. She said? I really needed to learn whether she was more of a single gestalt entity or they were a collective. 'We'll recon- vene to hear the witness's testimony at the usual time after lunch. All subsequent witnesses will be delayed by around an hour.'

———

We filed back into the room about two hours later. Joker stood absolutely rigid. Beneath her flimsy jerkin, every muscle in her back clenched as the defecting equidae resumed her place on the stand. Their side must have had a lot riding on the surgeon's testimony.

Violet waggled her furry tentacles in what I took to be a

general greeting to the room. 'Everyone, please take your seat. The time we lost this morning will make today's session run over so let's not waste time.' She gestured to the witness. 'Please, speak your piece.'

The surgeon tapped her hooves and began her speech. 'Good afternoon. My name is [no frame of reference]. Until today, I was a neonatal surgeon at the Happy Families Clinic in [no frame of reference] on Hwin. I have performed count-less penna-arthrectomies over the course of my career. The vast majority of these have been on newborns; however, in a small but not insignificant percentage of cases, the wings grow back.'

Joker's entire back flinched at that.

The surgeon licked her lips. 'Almost a third of people who have their wings removed at birth have to have a second procedure – usually around adolescence. In around ten per cent of cases, the wings grow back a second time. But in a tiny number of people, the wings grow back again and again. I have one patient whose wings have been removed no less than thirty-seven—'

'Hem-hem. Kindly stop saying these things. This is not why you're here. We didn't bring you light years from home to hear these lies.'

The thing about universal translators is that directional hearing goes out the window. All voices are directly in my earpiece, so I can never tell where a voice is coming from. That's why it took me a moment to figure out where the outburst came from. Apparently, it took the magistrates a few seconds as well. They were all looking around the room and conferring with each other.

They appeared to figure it out at the same moment I did. 'Joker, you will be silent or you will leave this place. Your outburst is not acceptable,' said the horta.

Violet raised a few furry tentacles. 'If you would like to be added to the list of witnesses, we will consider your application.'

Joker's tail swished in a way that would have meant anxiousness in Spock. I didn't know what it meant in equidae body language. 'No, tizzes,' she said. 'Not at this time. I apologise for my interruption.' She sat back down, still smiling.

Fern addressed the surgeon. 'Please continue, surgeon.'

She swallowed. 'I wasn't… I didn't mean to imply that the patient in question was present in this courtroom. I…' She chewed her lips thoughtfully. 'This … particular patient comes in once a year to have the surgery performed. I am an award-winning orthopaedic surgeon – I like to think I'm good at what I do. Or what I did, I suppose. I guess I'll need to think about a new vocation.'

She tilted her head. 'I should have considered that before I did this. Still… No regrets.' She breathed in slowly. 'Anyhow, I told her she couldn't keep doing this. She has so much scar tissue in the area that each procedure is more difficult and riskier than the last. She must be in continuous pain.'

———

On the final day of witness testimony, Joker tossed her long auburn mane back over her shoulder and said, 'Good morning, tizzes. The petitioners have a request to submit. We apologise for the lateness of this; however, a witness we had invited became available only at the last minute and only for a very short window of time. You should receive the paperwork right about now.'

The person to her left tapped a few buttons on her tablet then looked back up.

The magistrates leant into one another and whispered for a few seconds.

On our side, the challengers were doing whispers of their own. *Frantic* whispers. They appeared to be furiously disagreeing. But with their privacy shield in place, I couldn't hear any of it. Zippy was grinding her teeth and Bungle was kicking the floor. Scully was aggressively hopping up and down. And Robocop ... she stood still ... in a threatening sort of manner.

After a few moments, Bungle stood up straight. 'Learned tizzes, we have to protest this move. This witness...' She shook her head. 'We believe her testimony will add nothing to these proceedings, serving only to further inflame an already fraught situation. Her presence here can only add to my client's distress.'

The bees replied, 'We permitted you extra time yesterday to deal with the unexpected defection of the surgeon. As such, it can only be fair to permit this. I'm sorry – but your objections are denied. The witness will join us. Please bring her in.'

Zippy turned around and whispered 'I'm so sorry' in Storm and Bexley's direction. We all looked back as the courtroom door slid open. A tall chestnut blond equidae walked in. She looked so much like Bexley it would have been impossible to miss the connection. Everyone in the room gasped – except Bexley, who whimpered softly.

'Daddy?'

The room filled with the susurrus of dozens of whispered conversations. Once again, I couldn't make out what anyone was saying.

'Silence,' said Fern. 'If the members of the audience will not be calm, they will be ordered to leave.'

A hush fell over the room as the light brown equidae took

the stand. She faced the room with a warm, charismatic smile. 'Good afternoon. I am [no frame of reference] and I'm the owner of Firefly, the engine manufacturing company.' *Ah. That dad.* 'The parent at the heart of this case is one of my ex-spouses. The child she's carrying now is not mine. But we do have three children together. Most people don't know this but...' She looked away into the distance for a moment before continuing. 'One of my children – one of the ones I share with Storm – suffers from the disorder.'

My hand shot up to my mouth. For a second, I thought I might be sick again but I held it in. The whispers around the room picked up again and multiple people started tapping away on their phones or tablets. A sharp look from Fern stilled everyone. Several of the hovering cameras flashed.

Bexley stared at the floor. Storm, Jean, and Peggy all crowded around her, holding her and hiding her from the cameras. I slid my hand into a narrow gap between Peggy and Jean and rested my hand on Bexley's fur. Spock wedged her way into the group and lay her head on Bexley's lap.

'We were living away from Hwin for a period when our middle child began exhibiting signs of the disorder.' The interpreted words were spoken directly into my right ear via the earbud I wore. In my left ear, I could hear Bexley quietly sobbing. 'It was a very trying time for our family. Storm suggested we not transfer her to a comfort resort. She thought we should try to manage her at home – as if the six of us could somehow magic up the skills to cope with her needs. We had two other children to think of.'

She tossed her head, her blond mane flowing gracefully. 'It was a stressful time for the whole family. So stressful. In the end, we couldn't agree on what to do. We ended up going our separate ways. Three of us stayed together and our other two children remained with us. We maintained a good relationship with two of our former spouses. But one' – she gestured at Storm – 'took our child and disappeared. In the middle of the night, she just … left. I haven't spoken to Storm since.'

The courtroom was silent – except for Bexley's sobs.

After a few moments, Bexley's parent continued. 'As for my special needs child, of course I still love her – we all do. But, well, she's a handful. She shows up every few months or she calls, always needing our help. The last time she called it was with some wild story about having been kidnapped. She wanted me to buy her a ship. From what I gather, she's found some people to take care of her. I suppose they must be better equipped to manage her needs than we are.'

She dabbed her eyes with a tissue before continuing. 'I love my child. But she'd be better off in a comfort resort. I have no doubt about that. They'd be able to deal with her outbursts and her inability to cope with things. Storm, her pouchy-parent, has always been too indulgent. She means well – just like I'm sure she means well with this newest child of hers. But she's too soft. She never did have the heart to say no. To stand up and do what's right for her children.'

Bexley burst from the room, bawling. The rest of us ran after her. Her other parents and Spock and me, that is. The last thing I caught as the door slid shut behind us was Bexley's horrible dad pointing at us and saying, 'You see what I mean? She always has to cause a scene.'

Outside, Storm called out, 'Bexley!'

Bexley paused but didn't turn around. 'What?' Her voice was soft and low.

Jean put her arms around her spouses. 'Do you want us to come with you?'

Bexley's shoulders fell. 'Yes. No. I don't… Thank you. I

think I'm just going to go back to the hotel.' She clasped my hand.

Her parents tapped their hooves in the air. 'Okay,' said Storm. 'We'll be at the flat if you want to come by later.'

I started to follow Bexley, then thought of something. 'Spock, can you walk Storm and her spouses home, please?' Storm wasn't supposed to go anywhere without protection until the hearing was finished.

'Spock protect.' She wagged her tail and headed off with Bexley's parents.

'Come on, you.' I put my arm around Bexley as we set out down the road. 'Let's get you back to the hotel. We can order drinks and watch a stupid film.'

Bexley snorted. 'I'm sorry you have to miss the rest of today's hearing because of me.' She reached up and touched the base of her missing horn. 'I really am useless.'

'No, you're definitely—' But then something hit me and I died.

Okay, so I wasn't dead – but I was warm and uncomfortable. I wasn't sure how long I'd been asleep, but I didn't feel refreshed. And was there something pinning me down? My face was smushed against a damp, hard surface. Either I'd been drooling or... Or something.

I'd been going somewhere, I thought. With someone. Everything was fuzzy though.

I tried to sit up but there was something on my back. Craning my neck, I tried to see what it was. 'Ow.' All I succeeded in was making myself dizzy. Instead, I reached around to feel what it was. 'Bexley? Are you sitting on me?'

She made some noises in response, but nothing Holly could translate into English.

I looked around the ... bridge? Were we back on the *Teapot*? Hadn't we been ... somewhere else?

'Bexley, what's happening?' My voice sounded muddled and raw.

'Gimme the salad,' muttered Bexley. 'On a plate.'

I thumped the heel of my hand into my forehead and tried to force this situation to make sense. I failed.

Bexley's weight lifted off my back with a sound that was probably a sharp intake of breath. Words tumbled out of her even faster than normal. 'What are we doing? How did we get here? Why are we on the bridge? Have we been kidnapped again? Who's taken us? Where are we going? Can someone get me something to eat – I'm absolutely famished.' She ran in circles around the bridge.

Without her weight pinning me in place, I sat up and looked around. We were indeed on the bridge of the *Teapot*. Specifically, on the floor of the bridge.

'Hem-hem. I was wondering when you two would wake up.' It took me a second to place the voice. Joker.

She was sitting at the pilot's station – at Henry's station. Her mane was loosely plaited and she wore the same mint green jerkin she'd worn at the hearing that day. 'The hearing,' I said.

Joker waved a hoof dismissively. 'Yes, we'll be missing the end of that. But it's been clear to me since almost the start that it was all a sham. You're obviously in collusion with the magistrates. The whole thing is a fraud. A farce. You make a mockery of our laws, our society, our history. Even science itself. Everything.'

I should've said something then but my mind was still fuzzy from the knockout drugs.

She snorted out a laugh. 'Why am I even telling you this? It's obviously not the pair of you organising anything. A unicorn and an animatronic tree? You couldn't even organise a sandwich.'

Joker stopped and looked Bexley straight in the eye. 'Oh, that's right. I know what you are. I know all about you. I've had my suspicions for a while but your parent's testimony today... Now that's a good parent. You should be thankful for her.'

I expected Bexley to fight back, to argue, to something... But she had her knees curled up to her chest and she stared at the floor.

'How dare you.' My brain was finally kicking back into gear. Kicking through treacle. But at least it was moving. 'You don't know her. You don't know us. A parent who betrays her child's trust doesn't deserve the name parent. Bexley is the smartest, strongest, best person I know. She's kind and generous and brave and loyal. Her parent lied on the stand. Or she doesn't know her at all. One or the other.'

Joker addressed Bexley. 'Leave it to a unicorn to develop an unnatural relationship with a tree. You disgust me. It pretends to love you. But you ... you're nothing but a worthless unicorn. If you were my child, I wouldn't have taken you to a comfort resort – I'd have dropped you off a cliff. The resorts are too good for the likes of you.'

Her venom caught me by surprise. It shouldn't have, but it did. The thin veneer of kindness and reasonableness of people like her invariably hid a heart full of hate. 'Where are you taking us?'

In the time-honoured tradition of unpleasant people everywhere, she spoke to me slowly and loudly with lots of odd pauses. 'We' – she waved her hoof between the three of us – 'are going' – flying away gesture – 'away from that perverse, godforsaken moon – that haven for groomers and child abusers.'

I rubbed my head. 'That's *why* we're leaving. I asked *where* we're' – I paused to make a walking gesture with my fingers – 'going to.' Two could play at that game.

Joker's grin was wide and more than a bit manic looking. 'Oh, it doesn't matter where we're going.' She continued the 'English tourist on holiday' routine in the way she spoke to me.

I needed to check on Bexley. Why wasn't she talking? Keeping my eyes on Joker, I scuttled on my bum across the floor to where Bexley had settled. Brushing her forelock from her face, I looked her in the eye. 'Are you okay?'

She swung her head away, refusing to look me in the eye.

'No, of course you're not all right. Obviously. But I mean, did she hurt you? Physically.'

She wouldn't answer or look at me. Being outed against her will was her worst nightmare. But to her childhood hero… That had to add a whole extra layer of pain. Not to mention what she went through with her horrible dad this afternoon.

I dropped down next to her – close enough to touch but letting her guide how much contact she was comfortable with at that moment.

Joker walked over and looked at us, a beatific smile spreading across her face. 'This closeness… The pair of you. It would be touching … if it weren't so perverse. You're disgusting.' Smile like an angel – sting like a prick.

I looked up at her. The last of the drug-induced haze had faded. The only thing coursing through my blood was venom and rage. 'I'll ask again,' I said through gritted teeth. 'Where are you taking us?'

Joker turned the smile down a notch. 'I wasn't joking. It really doesn't matter where we're going.' The blood drained from my face as I realised the implication of that statement. She sneered. 'I'm only doing what needs to be done in order to preserve the natural order of things. I'm not a monster. Surely you can see that.'

I felt like I was going to be sick. 'What?'

'Look, I'm being very reasonable,' she said, being entirely unreasonable. 'You clearly come from a scienceless people, so it's probably no surprise that you're finding this difficult to grasp.'

My breathing sped up. I had to slow it down. *Two, three, five, seven, eleven, thirteen.* Bexley needed me. And for that, I had to retain my wits. *Seventeen, nineteen, twenty-three, twenty-nine, thirty-one, thirty-seven.* 'All this because you're ashamed of your wings?'

The mask of sweetness fell away from her face for a second. But only for a second. 'I've no idea what you're referring to.'

'You.' I held out a hand, gesturing at her. 'You're the one that surgeon was talking about – the one whose wings keep growing back. It's nothing to be ashamed of, you know. You don't have to wear that waistcoat. You could own your uniqueness. You're a pegasus. Just go with it.' My imminent death had apparently emboldened me.

Joker breathed forcibly out through her nose. For several heartbeats, she stood there, glaring at me. Then she walked closer and squatted down in front of us, fixing her eyes squarely on Bexley. 'I care about you, Bexley. That's probably difficult for you to see right now. Well' – she tossed her braided mane over her shoulder – 'people like you find many things hard to comprehend. But especially right now in this moment. You may not see it but I'm doing this for your own good.'

A chill ran through me and something snapped. 'You literally just finished telling us you're going to kill us before we get where we're going.'

Joker stopped and studied me like I was a particularly recalcitrant puppy. 'Of course I'm not going to kill you, you strange person. What do you take me for?'

I took her for a cruel person driven to rid the galaxy of

difference. But right then I was mainly just confused. 'But… What?'

'Time's almost up.' She smiled sweetly … and punched herself in the face. Her lip split, leaking purple blood down onto her chest and gilet.

I screamed. Scrambling to get Bexley and me away from her, I demanded, 'What are you doing?'

'Only what's strictly necessary.' She grabbed her mane and yanked a chunk out. Ripped it right out of her skin.

As I gawped at her, she grasped her jerkin in her hooves and tore it. I screamed. And then she repeated the process, adding a second smaller tear on the other side. With each movement, I flinched and jerked.

'What? Why? What are you doing? Stop!' My hands shot up to my face.

I elbowed Bexley. 'Look!' But she still wouldn't engage.

Joker bashed her elbow on the pilot's station, emitting a horrible crunching sound. 'Oh, don't worry, dear. I'd never hurt you. I'm not a monster.' My stomach turned as blood smeared and sprayed and flowed.

The room spun around me – though I was pretty sure that this time it wasn't the sedatives.

With a screeching crash and the sound of tearing metal, I was thrown forwards, slamming my head on the floor. I hadn't felt anything like that since … since… 'Holly, what the holy hell just happened?'

'The *Teapot* has been forcibly docked with in flight,' it replied.

'By whom?'

But I knew the answer even before it said anything. 'The *Hat*.'

'Bastards.'

Something clicked in Bexley. She leapt up and ran for the

lift. Joker and I followed, squeezing in before the door slid shut.

'Hwin vessel the *Hat* to the criminals aboard the starship *Teapot*,' announced an unfamiliar voice. 'Stand down and prepare to be boarded. Release your hostage now and you will not be harmed.'

I looked at Joker, who smiled cloyingly through bleeding lips. One of her teeth hung at an odd angle. The door slid back open on the docking bay level.

An eerie silence blanketed the ship as we marched towards the docking bay door – where eight cops awaited us.

'I'm Bexley, captain of the *Teapot*, and this is our Director of Operations. We're unharmed. I'm hopeful that—'

'Resistance is futile,' one of the cops shouted – the same person who'd spoken while we were on the lift. 'Set your weapons down, *Teapot* crew.'

'What?' I blinked. 'We haven't got any weapons.'

'Aren't you here to rescue us?' Bexley asked.

'Oh, thank heavens you're here,' cried Joker, running past us. 'I've been ever so worried. It was so frightening. It's only dumb luck they didn't think to remove my communicator with its tracking device.' She positioned herself behind one of her officers.

'*Your* captors?' cried both Bexley and I in unison.

Bexley held her hooves up in front of herself. 'I don't know what's happening here but I'm sure we can get it all sorted out once we're back on Lagash.'

'Oh, you won't be going back to Lagash,' said the lead cop. 'Assault and kidnapping of a Hwin law enforcement officer is—'

Joker peered around the cop's shoulder and grinned at us. 'Save your breath, Detective Inspector. She's a unicorn, you know. Strong as an ox but not very bright. I suspect the one who looks like a cactus organised the crime — not that she's much smarter than her co-conspirator. Hence why you were able to catch them so easily.'

Bexley raised her hooves in a sort of placating gesture. 'We didn't kidnap anyone – I swear. Joker kidnapped *us*. Shot us with knockout drugs when we were—'

'She speaks really well.' The Detective Inspector looked at Joker, presumably her boss.

'I'm right here.' Bexley's voice croaked on the last word.

'I wonder who trained her,' the DI said. 'Do you think she understands what she's saying?'

'Er, hi.' I bent at the waist and tried to get the attention of the cops. 'We didn't kidnap Joker. She kidnapped us. If you're going to arrest us, don't we have rights? Like, a lawyer maybe? Because I want to talk to Bungle right now.'

'The alien will be silent,' barked the DI. 'Prisoners' rights will be accommodated once we arrive back on Hwin.'

'We did not kidnap or injure anyone.' Bexley spoke slowly and enunciated each syllable.

'Hold it right there and prepare to be boarded,' came a new voice, one with a thick Scottish brogue.

We must have stopped moving because instead of a screeching, tearing crash, I felt the usual dull thud of docking.

Moments later, Robocop's voice filled my ear again. 'Who's in charge here?'

A second after that, a black and russet blur flew through the air and into my arms. 'Lem! Lem safe!' Spock covered my face in sloppy kisses. At thirty-six kilograms, she was a lot for me to carry though, so I did my best to control her slide back to the floor.

She'd been followed from the *Teapot*'s other docking bay door by Robocop, Storm, and Bungle. And a few people of varying species who I suspected were Lagash cops. Storm hugged Bexley as ferociously as Spock had hugged me.

Joker smiled sweetly while clutching her now swollen elbow. 'The *Teapot* has been designated a crime scene and the *Hat* is my ship, Constable Robocop. And I would like to know what right you have to board either one. In fact, I'll have to insist you leave so we can transport these criminals to Hwin for sentencing.'

'Aye, and I'd like a wee dram of industrial-grade lubricant – but it's nae going to happen at this juncture either. Oh, and it's Commissioner Robocop if we're being all formal like. I'm afraid you' – she jabbed a purple truncheon in Joker's direction – 'are under arrest for the kidnapping and forcible detainment of two GU citizens, namely Bexley and Lem.'

The DI stepped closer to Robocop. 'What on Hwin are you talking about? It's plainly evident that Joker was kidnapped by these two creatures, not the other way around. We're on their ship and Joker is the only one here who's been injured.'

'She did that to herself,' said Bexley. 'We were all sitting there talking and all of a sudden she punched herself in the face and tore her vest. Tell them, Lem.'

The DI crossed her arms over her chest. 'Oh, did she really? And why would she—'

Robocop cut her off. 'As it happens, it doesnae matter whether Joker injured herself or if there was a scuffle with her victims—'

'These brutes assaulted *me*.' Joker batted her long eyelashes. 'I stepped outside the hearing to see if she' – Joker waved a hoof in Bexley's direction – 'was all right. I shouldn't have done – I knew what a risk I was taking. Even though it was absolutely right for Bexley's parent to testify, I was worried about how it would affect the poor misguided soul.

People like her may not understand much but they're capable of feelings. I just wanted to check in on her – but her ogre shot me full of drugs and dragged me to their ship. Who knows where they would have taken me if my team hadn't shown up. I'm the victim here.'

"Course you are, my lovely,' said Bungle. 'Of course you are.' If anyone could out-syrup Joker, it was Bungle.

Robocop continued as if neither Joker nor Bungle had interrupted. 'What matters is that Joker and one of her officers were recorded firing knockout weapons at Bexley and Lem and dragging their unconscious forms to a waiting getoff.'

The colour drained from Joker's face for just a second. 'What?'

'You did nae even consider we might have CCTV, did ye?'

'I'm innocent,' Joker wailed.

'Aye, sure ye are.' Robocop gestured at Joker and one of the other Hwin cops. Two of the Lagash officers slapped handcuffs on their wrists. 'My officers will get the two kidnappers back to our ship and safely stowed in the brig. DI, I hope you understand why your entire squad is under suspicion and, as such, my team and I will be taking over command of your ship. I'll ask you and your officers to confine yourselves to quarters. When we get back to Lagash, you'll be questioned. Assuming the rest of you weren't involved in the conspiracy, you'll be free to go.'

The DI's jaw fell slack but she tapped her hooves in the air and ordered her officers to follow her.

'Well, then,' said Bungle. 'I suppose we ought to turn this party around and head back to Lagash. Zippy messaged me half an hour ago to say closing arguments were concluded. It's all over until the magistrates make their decision.'

We walked back into court the morning the magistrates were expected to give their decision. All of us except Joker, that is. She was in custody, awaiting a hearing of her own.

Two days had passed since we'd left the hearing – and Bexley and I had gone on our little adventure.

The energy in the room felt more nervous than excited. People were mingling and speaking in hushed tones. Cameras hovered, snapping pics and recording holos of everyone present – especially Bexley and me.

Bexley and Storm clung to one another. Storm could be sent back to Hwin and her baby operated on without her consent. For that matter, Bexley, Jean, and Peggy could all be extradited to face charges of aiding and abetting child abuse. And if Bexley was sent to Hwin, she'd be sent to a comfort resort.

My heart raced. I had to be strong for Bexley – but I didn't know if I had it in me. Dropping to the floor, I put my arms around Spock.

She sniffed at my face then studied me. 'Lem okay?'

I wondered, not for the first time, how much of these

proceedings she understood. With my hands in her thick fur, I breathed deep. 'I'm not okay right now, mate. But I hope I will be soon. I hope we *all* will be.'

A hush descended on the room as the magistrates strode in and took their seats.

'Thank you all for joining us today,' said Violet in her soft, delicate voice. 'I'm sure you will appreciate that this case – much like every case we hear – is a difficult one. While the GU has a mandate to uphold person rights, we also have a duty to respect the sovereignty of member planets and their individual states. At the start of this hearing, we told you our decisions rarely please either the petitioners or the challengers. And this case will be no exception.'

The room buzzed with a murmuring of clicks and raspberries – equidae whispers. My throat tightened.

Fern allowed people a few moments to digest what she'd said before she picked up the thread. 'We have listened to the witness testimony, the opening and closing remarks of both counsels. We have also reviewed the documentary evidence submitted by both sides. Additionally, we have received letters from thousands of people across the GU. We offer you our assurances that everything submitted has been taken into account.'

Fern waved a frond to indicate the horta, who spoke next. 'The four of us have reviewed and debated these matters extensively and discussed them with members of the galactic parliament. Taking all that into account, our unanimous decision is as follows. We find that if Hwin chooses to remain a member of the GU, certain changes will be required. Hwin laws mandating skeletal modification are not in keeping with the GU charter of rights and freedoms.'

All around the room, equidae were leaping and knocking hooves with one another. Given that they were mostly people who lived here, I assumed they were cheering. Some of the journalists looked less pleased. I was wary.

'If I may finish,' rumbled the rock-person. 'Hwin laws mandating skeletal modification are not in keeping with the GU charter of rights and freedoms. Moreover, laws requiring the incarceration of skelediverse persons do not respect the rights of those individuals. Additionally, in order for Hwin to continue as a member of the GU in good standing, skelediverse people must be recognised as full citizens with all the rights, freedoms, and responsibilities that come along with that in an advanced society.'

The cheering started up again – but the horta wasn't finished.

My stomach did that thing where it felt like the bottom was about to drop out. I could sense a *but* coming.

'But having said all that, Hwin remains sovereign and we will not place conditions upon the Hwin government *permitting* these acts. They must not be required, but nor should they be forbidden. Each family, each parent, must decide for themselves what is right.'

The cheers fell away and a hush descended over the room.

It was the bees who spoke next. 'A written copy of our decision will be made available to the public within the next few minutes. Thank you.'

I inhaled, taking my first deep breath in what felt like weeks. That wasn't as bad as I'd feared.

The four magistrates stood and departed the room without another word.

Bexley turned her face up towards me. 'That's a victory, right? Like, it's a start at least?'

I put my arm around her. 'Yeah, I think it is.'

———

Zippy, Bungle, Scully, and Robocop all walked into a pub. That's not a joke – it's just what happened.

Jean nodded at them as they sat. 'Thank you – all of you – for your hard work on this case. The decision today means we're not criminals. You've saved our baby's wings.'

Zippy tapped two hooves on the edge of the table as she took a seat. 'You're welcome, of course. But this wasn't just a win for your family. The Hwin government couldn't have extradited me – since I couldn't have survived the surgery. But Bungle... If she'd been forced to go back, I would have gone with her and fought for her freedom. For the rest of my life if need be.'

'So would I,' added Robocop. She stretched out an implement that looked like a spork and stroked Bungle's arm.

Storm clutched her belly with one hoof while leaning against Peggy. 'I just feel so bad that we brought all this trouble to Lagash. It's such a beautiful society you've all built here. And because of us, thousands of people could have been forced from their homes.'

Bexley crossed her arms over her chest. 'No.'

All eyes turned to her – even Spock, who'd awoken at the sound of her voice.

Bexley pushed her forelock down over her long nose. Immediately, she seemed to think better of it as she brushed it off her face, revealing the bare stump of her horn. 'It was about us and about your baby and – oh, I'm going to start crying.' She waved her hooves in front of her face. 'Happy tears – I promise. Lem, you tell them what you told me earlier.' She snorted.

Right. I wrapped my arm around her. 'When I first met Bexley, I had a reaction to her – a physical reaction, I mean.

My body stopped breathing. I nearly died. It was lucky BB was on the ship because she saved me. In fact, if I wasn't taking the medicine she created for me, I wouldn't be able to sit here with you all now.'

Around me, the facial expressions, body language, and colour coding conveyed confusion.

I pressed on. 'It was Bexley who taught me the value and importance of acceptance. She welcomed me. In fact, the whole *Teapot* crew did. BB made medicine for me. Aurora worked to understand complex and sometimes contradictory human dietary preferences and made clothes for me, even though she didn't understand why I needed them. Bexley made shoes for me. Henry built furniture sized for me. Everyone on that ship simply accepted that I was unlike other people they knew. They didn't begrudge me. They didn't expect me to accommodate my own needs. They simply welcomed me and made adjustments accordingly.'

Bexley squeezed my hand. Zippy leant into Bungle and rested a hoof on Robocop's lid.

'Lagash is a community,' I continued. 'And a community works best when its members choose to embrace one another and work together to support the whole – even if they've been thrown together by accident. I've only been here a couple of weeks, but I get the sense that's exactly what Lagash is all about.'

Zippy and Bungle both tapped their hooves on the table and Scully nodded, her long ears bobbing with each movement.

I turned to Storm. 'And you raised a hell of a wise offspring. Her other dad was both right and wrong about her life on the *Teapot*. In a way, we do support her and accommodate her – but no more so than she does for us. Just as we all do for one another.'

Aurora glowed green. 'Hear, hear. Very wise words, my young friend.'

BB's pupils expanded and contracted as she fluffed the feathers on her face.

From behind us came a voice I didn't recognise. 'Oh, you have got to be kidding me!'

A group of equidae were gathered at a table a few metres away. A second voice added, 'Back that up a couple of minutes and put it on the big holo. Everyone should hear this.'

A plump grey equidae appeared in the centre of the pub. '...results released this morning showed that, despite the change to the laws, ninety-four per cent of people would still opt for the procedure if their infant was found to have the defect. And eighty-three per cent would choose to surrender their child to a comfort resort if she were found to have the disorder. [No frame of reference] is talking to people on the streets of—'

The pub erupted in annoyed shouting and grumbling. I caught little snatches of people's words. 'Can't believe' and 'after everything' and 'ableist crap'. I shook my head. It was different from anything I'd experienced on Earth ... and yet achingly familiar.

Jean neighed. 'I'm sorry. And I don't want to be the cynic or the pessimist or whatever, but the outcome was never going to be better than this. If they'd outright banned comfort resorts and infant surgery, Hwin would have declared war on the GU. It's not a war they could win ... but they genuinely believe they're right in this. They would rather turn even more inward and isolationist than be forced into a change they're not ready for.'

She clasped the hooves of her two spouses and pulled them together. 'By granting unicorns and pegasuses and other skelediverse people full citizenship, change *will* come. Eventually. It may be a long time coming. But it will happen.'

Zippy reached across the table and added her hoof to the pile. 'You are far from pessimistic, Jean. In fact, I wish I shared your optimism. I'm not sure things will change for people like us on Hwin – at least not in our lifetime. In the short term, they may get worse as people exact revenge for forcing change on them.'

Bungle lovingly punched her spouse on the arm. 'Excuse my darling. She may be beautiful but the universe has never produced a more melodramatic cynic.' They shared a small kiss and then Bungle took a sip of her carrot wine. She cast a sideways glance around the table. 'Come on then, my lovelies … who had Joker down as a secret pegasus?'

We carried on drinking and talking. Laughing and commiserating and relaxing. A few hours later, Bexley excused herself to take a call.

'Oh my gosh, everyone. You're not going to believe it. That was Megaboulder! The Accountants of Doom are two planets into their galactic tour and their space coach has to bail on them at their next stop. She saw the news of the hearing and she said she's even more excited than ever about wanting to work with us. She wants to know if we can meet her on Quoth and take over. It would keep us busy for the next six weeks – but we have to leave first thing tomorrow. What do you say? Should we do it?'

## THE END (FOR NOW)

Thank you for reading *Consider Pegasus*, the third book in the *Starship Teapot* series.

Sign up to my newsletter you'll get updates on what I'm working on, pet pics, book reviews, and free stories. If you'd like to read about Lem's life on Earth – including how she first met Spock – click below.

PSST! WANT A FREE BOOK?

Click the image above to get Jurassic Dark for free

## ACKNOWLEDGEMENTS

Towards the end of 2020, I decided I just … couldn't. I couldn't face another serious novel about serious people dealing with serious problems.

And so instead, I sat down to write something excessively silly. That something silly turned into *The Left Hand of Dog*, the first book in the *Starship Teapot* series.

And then the second book, *Judgement Dave*, came out much darker than I'd intended. How does a person try to write a bit of lightweight, easy-reading space opera only to have it turn into an essay about slavery, genocide, and oppression?

I don't know – but that's exactly what happened.

So, of course, for the third book, I sat down once again to write a bit of silly fluff. I worked on that book for eight solid months and only managed to squeeze out about a third of a novel before I finally called it a day. And then I started over with a new story and… Oops, I did it again. This book is every bit as dark as the second.

I worked hard to get the balance right: the darkness of the themes and the lightness of the tone. My aim is always to address real issues but to do so in a way that has warmth and heart – that respects the sanctity of life and the rights of people. I want to write stories that are diverse and inclusive at their very core.

Did I achieve those aims? I hope so, but I'm sure some of

you will say no. If your reasons for disliking this story include the terms 'political correctness' or 'SJW', then ... shrug. You're not my audience. On the other hand, if you didn't like this story because you think it should have been more inclusive or because I should have tried harder to avoid the white saviour trope, I'd love to hear from you. I'm always striving to learn more, to do better, to *be* better than I was yesterday. Please get in touch.

Tongue firmly wedged in cheek, I'd like to thank J.K. Rowling for providing the inspiration for Joker. Joker is *not* her ... but, well, let's just say she fed my muse.

As always, the WiFi Sci-Fi writers' group has been the most amazing gift. They continually teach, push, and cheer-lead me to be a better writer.

This time, I've also got a new group to thank: Bright Future. We're a group (or should that be gronp?) of indie authors committed to writing diverse and inclusive sci-fi. We support one another with the business side of authoring ... which, let me tell you, is hard work. I owe my thanks to everyone in the group for their support and guidance.

I want to thank Isabelle Felix, my beta reader, and Charlie Knight, my developmental editor. They both got stuck right into the guts of my ridiculous tale – revealing the flaws, pointing out where I'd done exactly what I said I was trying to avoid, drawing out the details I'd invariably glossed over, and asking me all the right questions. I highly recommend them both.

Nick Taylor of Just Write Right dug into the meat of this vegetarian story to make it the best version of itself it could be. And, as always, Hannah McCall of Black Cat Editorial Services provided expert proofreading. Any mistakes you find now are because I forgot to incorporate her corrections.

Finally, my legally contracted lifemate, Dave, has been

putting up with more than any human being should have to. If you've ever met me in real life, you'll understand what a big deal that is. Seriously … I'm *a lot*. Dave has listened to me talk about my imaginary friends every single day for five years. Dave's the best person.

## ABOUT THE AUTHOR

Photo © Liza O'Malley

SI CLARKE is a misanthrope who lives in Deptford, *sarf ees* London. She shares her home with her partner and an assortment of waifs and strays. When not writing convoluted, inefficient stories, she spends her time telling financial services firms to behave more efficiently. When not doing either of those things, she can be found in the pub or shouting at people online – occasionally practising efficiency by doing both at once.

As someone who's neurodivergent, an immigrant, and the proud owner of an invisible disability, she strives to present a realistically diverse array of characters in her stories.

Find her mostly on Mastodon these days.

twitter.com/clacksee

instagram.com/clacksee_author

goodreads.com/clacksee

bookbub.com/authors/si-clarke

facebook.com/clacksee

## ALSO BY SI CLARKE

Find a complete list of my books on my website at
whitehartfiction.co.uk/books.

If you get books directly from me, you'll get 20% off with the code
'WEBSITE'.

### REVIEWS

If you enjoyed this story, please consider leaving a review on
Goodreads, Readerly, or the ebook retailer of your choosing.

### KEEP IN TOUCH

Join my newsletter for:

- snippets from what I'm working on;
- photos of my dogs;
- reviews of books I've enjoyed recently;
- links to promos focusing on diverse and inclusive
  speculative fiction; and
- more free stories from me.

whitehartfiction.co.uk/newsletter-1